Dedication

This book is dedicated to the memory of
Police Inspector Joseph Vaughn—a genuine colleague,
brother, and friend to those who knew him.

He was dedicated to service and in the end
succumbed to its enormity.

You will keep Him in perfect peace,
Whose mind is stayed on You,
Because He trusts in You. Isaiah 26:3

Acknowledgments

This book would not be realized without the support and input of others, whether directly or indirectly, and it is with that spirit in mind I would like to extend my most sincere and infinite appreciation to my family and friends who played a part in its creation.

Thank you to Rachel Merritt for her cover design and interior formatting.

Last but not least I want to say thanks to my Editors, Tracy Liebchen and Virginia Havely; your invaluable work is recognized and profoundly appreciated.

CONTENTS

CHAPTER ONE

A man lay dead at the end of a dusty roadway near Grove Street. The lonely trail peaked at the pinnacle of the modest hillside and then plateaued. Apart from nearby trees swaying gracefully in the delicate breeze and curious flies that seemed fascinated with the decedent's eyes, nothing else showed signs of life. The irreversible reality of death raised its ugly head once again in Columbus, Ohio, and claimed its unfortunate casualty. To many, it remained a mystery. What motivates a man to hunt his own kind, like wolves in the wild? No crystal ball was required to predict it wasn't a good sign for Columbus. No mystery remained in anyone's mind whether this one was indeed a horrific homicide. The degree of cruelty involved made that fact abundantly obvious even to the blind.

The January morning was frosty cold with a pinch that chilled under the skin. A light, icy drizzle rode the feeble wind and made the morning dim. Some say time is the master of all things. On this occasion, the turning times delivered a horrific death to the city's doorsteps.

It was Detective Sergeant Alyssa Payne's first day back at work after soaking up a three-week vacation in the sunny State of Florida. She drove over the gritty gravel to the foot of the berm. Her partner, Detective Chris Toombs, immediately moved toward her with pen and notepad in hand. A couple of uniformed cops preserved the scene, which was cordoned off with evidence tape. The body laid supine on the dirt at the end of the road, beaten, bloodied, and broken. Back over the berm, the sparsely scattered trees stretched downhill and connected with the main thoroughfare at an intersection with Grove Street. Isolated and quiet, that location was paradise to those who wished to stay off the grid undetected.

"Welcome back, partner. You couldn't have picked a better day to return. Hope you had plenty of fun and sun because you're stepping right back into the graveyard," Toombs said.

"Might be a bit late for the dead guy, but at least he seems to be looking up. So, who is the stiff?" Alyssa asked.

"Fabian Davidson, twenty-nine years old with multiple priors. His rap sheet is as long as the River Nile.

Bonded out of County two days ago on drugs and robbery charges. Based on this massive overkill, someone really wanted to hurt him."

"Numerous prison tattoos all over; he was certainly a popular guy on the inside. What kind of tool do you think made these wounds? My guess, a sledgehammer or something equally solid," Alyssa said.

"Six fingers chopped off. They spared no cruelty with this guy. Doesn't seem like an attempt to conceal his identity, though."

"No, it doesn't. If the killer was trying to conceal his identity, he would have taken all the fingers, so that's not it. Perhaps he did it to complicate the investigation and buy time as he discarded the body like garbage. Get in touch with Vice and our guys at gang's intelligence. See if anything flies on their radar that connects to him," Alyssa said.

"Sure thing. Payne, you have no idea how happy I am that you're back. That schmuck Detective Biggs is a real piece of work. Can't wait to see the back of him. He's not a bad detective. He's just a weird one to work with."

"Come on, Biggs is one of the good guys. You just missed me, that's all. Davidson's phone, did you find it?"

"No. If he had one, it isn't here. We did a quick search before you arrived, and there was no sign of a phone."

"Well. The killer certainly wasn't beating around the bush with this one."

CHAPTER TWO

P ayne and Toombs arrived at homicide to a party-like atmosphere. Cheers of welcome back, and the sharing of cupcakes brought the office instant delight. McBride and Cruikshank stood at their desks in pleasant acknowledgment of her return, and so too did Greenwood and Hanson. High fives and cheeky jokes saw Alyssa out and down the hallway to Lieutenant Lorrigan's office. Lorrigan was still riding high on the massive serial killer case they closed a few months earlier in 2021. Since then, the Columbus Police Department could do no wrong in the eyes of the masses. For the most part, they were seen as the savior of the city, and Alyssa Payne was the primary reason.

"Aha, my star detective is back in business. Goddamn, Payne. All of a sudden, you're an overnight rockstar. Everybody wants a piece of you these days," Lorrigan said, leaning backward into the huge leather chair.

"I'm only here to do my job. Solving homicides is what I do, not playing a PR puppet. It may be good for the department, but I'll leave the politics to the guys who make the big bucks."

"Detective Biggs signed off on all the casefiles he worked on with Toombs while you were bathing in the sun. They're on your desk. Biggs went back to his division this morning. So, I see you caught a dead banger on your way in. How's that going?"

"Nothing yet, but we're eyeballing a few possibilities. Let you know what we find," Alyssa said, rising to her feet.

"Okay. I got to tell you, it's great that you're back with us again. I forgot to inquire. How's Daniel doing?" Lorrigan said.

"Dad's doing good, really good. He's tough," she concluded, then exited.

Alyssa traded Lorrigan's spacious office for her own, which was probably half the size and a lot less comfortable. She slid into the chair and tunneled head-on into the files on her desk. Three weeks away the office seemed a strange place to her. She stewed on the picture of her parents on the desk, staring back at her. Thoughts triggered deep within her of the innumerable changes she had experienced and how far she had come. Where life had landed them at that particular moment in time. Her magnificent gift for fighting crimes. It all seemed so reflectively nostalgic yet hopeful and refreshing simultaneously. It also presented an opportunity for brutal honesty of her take on the situation. All eyes were on her while the scope of expectations exploded tenfold. Many believed she was so shrewd she could simply wave her magic wand and miraculously solve murders. However, when all was said and done, she knew nothing was further from the truth. She had to work even harder than before. She now had to dig deeper and continue following the evidence wherever it went, regardless of whom it led to.

A slight rap bounced off the open door as Detective Hanson entered the office and dropped into a chair before Alyssa's desk. Hanson's commitment to the job had always been rock solid and even more so since joining Alyssa's team. Though Hanson loved being on the job, she could also be a bit of a firebrand at times. Consequently, it came as no surprise that she'd butted heads with Alyssa once or twice in the past, both being passionate in the way they expressed their views. In the end, butting heads took nothing from the mutual respect that existed between them.

"How was the trip?" Hanson asked.

"Better than expected. Plenty of bourbon and a whole lot of sleep. The night life was fun too, but you know I was never much of a fun junkie," Alyssa replied.

"It was a bit slow here, and Detective Biggs did okay, though there wasn't much to investigate in terms of murders. Until now anyway."

"I'm heading out to the deceased's residence. Was there something else you needed?" Alyssa asked.

"Just making sure you had a good time, but now I'm not so certain you did," Hanson said, followed by a parting giggle.

Alyssa headed out and joined her partner at his desk. Word came back from Vice and the gang unit, and as far as they could tell, nothing grabbed their attention regarding Davidson's killing. Alyssa and Toombs left the office bound for Fabian Davidson's home. It was believed he lived with his mother at Franklinton. Mere minutes cutting through traffic was all it required until they drew down at the gate. A couple of guys polished a car parked two houses down with the doors open and music thumping. Both detectives glanced at each other and then slipped through the gate onto the front porch.

Quick knocks on the door drew a curious-looking middle-aged lady to their aid.

"I don't need to ask who you're here for, do I? So, what did he do this time? Don't matter anyway because Fabian ain't here," she said, shifting her gaze between them.

"I'm Detective Payne, and this is my partner Detective Toombs. Please, may we come inside for a moment?"

She stepped out of the way and waved them in. "Already said Fabian wasn't here. I know, you're just doing your job, right? Detective, how am I doing so far?" the woman asked, pointing them to the couch.

"Are you Fabian's mother?"

"Yes, I'm his mother. It wasn't easy. Boy tried to come into the world the wrong way, but after three agonizing hours in labor, I gave birth to him. Did something happen? Is he okay?"

"I'm sorry to be the bearer of bad news, but Fabian was killed. He was found this morning."

A sorrowful silence swept across the room as reality settled in. The woman bowed her head and fought valiantly to deny her falling tears from drenching her stiffened cheeks, but she couldn't. She turned away from the detectives and glanced down at her folded hands in her lap. Then she raised her head and looked around the room, still avoiding the detectives. Something about her said she always knew this day would come. She simply didn't know when, and from the look of things, it probably hurt more than anything she had ever experienced.

"When did you see him last?" Toombs asked.

"He was locked up in County Jail for two long weeks, you know. If it had not been for the help of Pastor Goudy, he would still have been wasting away in that awful place. If I had just left him there, he would still be alive today. Pastor Goudy helped me bond him out on Saturday. He spent the night with me here and left around midday on Sunday. That was the last time I laid eyes on him," she said, mopping moisture from her face with a tissue.

"Did he mention anything about having a beef with anyone?"

"No."

"Can you think of anybody who would hurt your son? Anyone who wanted him dead?"

"Could be someone from the rotten crowd he ran with, or any of the folks he swindled. There is no denying he was terribly troubled, but he was still my son," she sobbed, bowing her head farther into the bulge of her bosom.

"Do you mind if we take a look around his room?"

"Down the hall, the door on the right."

The detectives made their way down the hall into the dark gray-painted room. Inside was as bare as a worn-out spare tire. A bed, a night table with signs of cigarette burns, and a half-empty closet. He clearly spent little time there, at least in that room anyway. Within minutes of entering the deceased's darkened den, they were right back out the door. When they exited the house, the men on the roadway were gone and so was the car with the thumping music.

"What do you think?" Toombs asked.

"What do I think about what?" Alyssa asked.

"You know. How this whole thing is shaping up for you? It's not awfully unusual for a guy with sticky fingers to get caught up, is it?"

"It's early days yet, and I haven't seen anything convincing one way or the other in terms of motive. Our next stop should be the medical examiner. Hopefully, he'll give us something to work with."

A quiet slow cruise carried them to the ME's office. As far as Toombs was concerned, Davidson led a crude street life of ruthless dishonesty, making enemies at every angle. His brutal battering and eventual demise most likely came as a result of a dubious deal gone wrong. Maybe he stiffed the wrong street dealer or robbed the wrong household and death was the price he paid. Should the detectives decide to straddle down the path of possible reprisals for his crimes, that list would be far too lengthy to unravel effectively. The number of people who'd suffered at his hands were innumerable. Still, it would only account for those reported, the unwritten ones could possibly prove even more vengeful and deadly.

T he medical examiner's office seemed as old and cold as always, which contrasted Doctor Sherman's lively personality. He laughed, grabbed the detectives' hands, and shook them hard then began unloading his monologue of praise and gratitude. He praised the Columbus Police Department, asserting that his bet was always posted on Payne's to solve the Jurist case. He plunged so deep into his animated stint that Alyssa had to steer him back on course to the issue at hand.

"What about the stiff that came in this morning, Fabian Davidson? What can you tell me about him?" Alyssa asked.

"Yes, of course, quite a bit, actually. Please, forgive my propensity to babble. I'm simply overjoyed to witness justice served to that monster while I'm still alive," Sherman said.

"Duly noted. I'm right there with you on that, Doc," Alyssa said.

Doctor Sherman led the way into the morgue, slipped on a pair of gloves, and made his way to the body laying supine on a table. Perhaps the chills of refrigeration penetrated the body and made the severity of the injuries appear more vividly. Whatever it was, the extent of the horrific beating became luminously apparent through his rigid skin. Toombs peered down at the deceased and then focused on Alyssa. Neither of these two detectives could be considered strangers to the sadness that hovered over dead bodies. Particularly in the case of homicides. That looming veil of tragedy always seemed to hang and hovered in the shadows. That was the harsh reality of their jobs. Even though detectives and doctors are trained professionals who learned early on not to make the cases personal, it was

easier said than done. No training in the world prevented them from being human.

"Come closer. Take a look here at all this bruising.
Shattered fibulas and badly bruised femurs. Nine broken ribs. Both arms broken at the radius which could
very well be defensive fractures. Three fingers snipped
from each hand probably by a garden clipper. See here,
the fatal blow came from his fractured skull. Death
didn't find him quickly; the killer made sure of it. All
this violence and rage brought this poor felon a world of
agony. I don't say this lightly, but in all my days of con-
ducting autopsies; I've never seen anything this cruel
and egregious." Doctor Sherman sighed and stared at
them.

"Any thoughts on the perpetrator or the type of
weapon?" Toombs asked.

"It took strength to break bones like this. So, he's
physically strong. The fingers were most likely removed
with some kind of clipper. As for the bulk of the damage,
that weapon was something heavy. Quite likely something blunted, something made of iron or hard wood.
At the scene, I noticed a small army of ants converged
on his lips and remaining fingers. That might explain a
thing or two down the road," the doctor said.

With that overview of his exterior observation, Doctor Sherman pressed the record button on his recording device. As the autopsy officially kicked into motion, Sherman spoke into the microphone, listing his findings in chronological order. He moved on to cutting the body open as he continued the examination of the interior. By the end, he concluded much of what was already known. Davidson suffered nine broken ribs and collapse lungs. He never stood a chance with his fractured femurs, tibias, humerus, and massive head trauma. There was no coming back from the rage of his killer. Whatever motivated the perpetrator, his extreme overkill made the murder appear personal. Sherman collected a sample from the stomach contents for analysis at the lab.

Chapter Three

Three happy horses grazed from the green acreage that encircled the ranch. Smoke from Daniel Payne's smoldering cigar circled and dissipated in the wind. Freshly percolated coffee steamed from his mug while he tapped his feet and watched the sun make its first appearance of the morning. With such a magnificent view from his porch, retirement finally felt like fun for him.

As far as he was concerned, his glory days were long gone, but Alyssa's were just taking shape. Nothing brought him more joy and satisfaction than to watch Alyssa work her way up the rugged rungs of the world. Alyssa descended the stairwell dressed and ready for work. She wore her brown boots, long-sleeved white shirt, and khaki-colored pants like a storefront model. A long, brown overcoat swung over her arm, and her Glock was at her waist.

"Coffee is hot, and I made eggs just the way you like them," Daniel said.

"Nice. Smells really good, Dad. I'll get it to go. How come you're in such a good mood this morning?" Alyssa asked.

"Let's just say I see things in a whole different perspective these days. I was out when you got home last night. I take it your first day back on the job went well?"

"If you consider a body dumped at a dead end a good day, then yes, it was a real doozey. Besides the body, it felt good getting my feet wet again. By the way, Lorrigan said hello, and so did Doctor Sherman."

"Oh, they probably thought I would be rolling in my grave by now."

"Dad, you're such a grouch. You know they mean well. They're friends, and they just want to know you're okay. Anyway, talk later," she said, then exited.

Coffee mug in hand, Alyssa stomped stridently through the office at homicide. The unmistakable kick of boots kissing tiles got everyone's attention for sure. The second floor had been reintegrated. It was opened up to accommodate the entire homicide contingent, not just Alyssa and her team. Notwithstanding the changes, as supervising detective, she still kept her office adjoining the open floor. Cubicles spanned both sides of the aisle that ran straight down the middle. The layout was fresh and practical. Though it didn't afford all the privacy of an office, it provided a reasonable environment for effective police work. A few potted plants added to the decor and brought freshness to the usual bare-bones police precinct background.

McBride snapped his fingers in the air while his other hand held the phone to his ear. Once the brief conversation concluded, he hung up and hesitated instead of announcing what he'd learned. After his deliberate demonstration of urgency, all eyes pointed squarely toward him. Somewhere within the mix of McBride's split-second pause, he appeared lost in distant thoughts. Alyssa always had a stare that seemed to cut clear through you, and she didn't hesitate to lay it on him.

"So, are you going to say something, or are you just going to sit there and wait for Christmas?" Alyssa said.

McBride batted his eyes a few times like he'd awoken from a dream. "They found another body in an alley off Humphrey Avenue. Crime scene is already en route."

"You alright, partner? You seem a little distracted. Is there something going on that I need to know about?" Cruikshank asked from his desk across from him.

"No. It's all good. Didn't get much sleep last night, that's all," McBride replied.

A lyssa and Toombs got in her Dodge truck and left for Humphrey Avenue. A few minutes later, they arrived at the scene. The shirtless body of a male laid prone on the asphalt beside an overflowing dumpster. The filthy alley sliced off Humphrey Avenue and ran behind an old plaza. Most of the shops there had closed except one restaurant called The Golden Spoon. The entire plaza was designated for renovation in the coming months and was almost completely deserted. A quick scan of the surroundings found no streetlights or cameras in the immediate environs.

A patrol unit awaited them along with Julius and his crime scene crew. A vehicle from the medical examiner's office pulled up and parked behind the line. As they moved in for a closer look, similarities to the previous murder gripped their attention like a vice.

"Detective Payne, good to see you and your protege as always," Doctor Sherman said.

"Good to see you too, though I hardly think my partner will take kindly to that title," Payne said.

"Aw, my good friend knew I meant no insult to his unquestionable expertise. Your VIC on the ground would have a lot more to complain about if he could," Sherman said.

Doctor Sherman marched right by them, turned, gave a swift salute, and then proceeded to the body. Though the victim's nose was still down in the dirt, they could tell it was a male. After observing for a few seconds, he indicated readiness to roll the body on its back. Despite the rigidity of the skin, both arms and legs slumped in whatever direction gravity demanded. Sherman immediately swung around and stared Alyssa in the eyes, and she reciprocated like clockwork. It seemed as if she read the doctor's mind. Whatever telepathic message was silently transmitted between them, their facial expressions confirmed it wasn't good.

"This wretched soul got the worst end of a blunt object. Almost every limb on his body broken. No question he was brutally beaten to death," Sherman said, turning his attention back to the body.

"How long?" Alyssa said.

Doctor Sherman reached for his thermometer, checked the body, and glanced at his watch before responding.

"I would say he has been dead somewhere between ten and twelve hours, somewhere between 10 p.m. and midnight. This massive fracture to the forehead is the most likely cause of death. Of course, you know this is all preliminary until I can properly examine him."

Sherman pulled a wallet from the dead man's pants pocket and handed it to Toombs. His driver's license gave his name as Brian Johnson, of Powell Avenue in Columbus. They ran him through the system, and his record played a full symphony. Alyssa initially thought she'd recognized him, but the blow to his skull initially made it a little tricky. Now she had confirmation that her intuition was spot on from the get-go. Johnson had been a thorn in cops' backs for well over a decade. Alyssa looked at his hands and saw that he still had all ten fingers, but the rest of his body was just as broken as the first victim. Johnson would have turned twenty-nine years old in three days on Friday, January 14th, but apparently, death was too impatient to wait that long.

In spite of the huge open wound to his head, there was no blood spatter or pooling near the body. So far, there was no indication that anyone witnessed the killing. The body was reported by the garbage truck driver who came to pick up trash and saw Johnson face down in the waste.

Alyssa snapped a couple of pics of the deceased and the alleyway on her mobile. She next called Hanson at the office and told her to dig into his background, including his next of kin and any known associates. With the gaping wound on the dead man's head and no pooling of blood or spatter anywhere, it was plausible the alley wasn't the scene of his demise. Payne gloved up and went through the decedent's pockets. She ran her fingers over the cuffs then leaned in and smelled it.

"What the hell is going on? I really hope this isn't some gang feud. Two career criminals dead in as many days. What are the odds they fell afoul of lousy luck?" Toombs said.

"Unless bad luck wields an iron or wooden bat, then I don't think that's what we're looking for here. We need to connect the dots between both men and see if they crossed paths. Let's see where things go from there. They might have gotten themselves mixed up with the wrong crowd, and somebody is cleaning house. Remember the days of the mob? They would ritualistically slice a finger off for any act of dishonesty or disloyalty. What if someone wanted to make an example of Davidson?" Alyssa asked.

"So, you think some kind of wise guy is making a play and shaking up business in the criminal world? The guys at gang intel came up completely empty. No chatter, not even so much as a murmur."

"I'm just saying, whatever is happening is playing out in our streets, and that's where the answers reside. Look for anything that doesn't belong here. Anything that may have been dumped here along with him. Everything about the body is key to telling us where he'd been and, if we're lucky, where he died."

"Okay, point taken. That restaurant may have been open last night; what you say we go check inside? We might get lucky; somebody may have seen or heard something."

A few strides took them to the Golden Spoon Restaurant, setting off musical chimes from the doorbell. A guy with crazy eyes seated near the door glanced at them then hurriedly shoveled down the last of his bacon and eggs. The pleasantness on the waitress's face dissipated the minute she turned and planted eyes on them. The less than five-star appearance inside perfectly explained why the plaza was preparing for a major makeover. In other words, the place was not exactly ritzy by any stretch of the imagination. Their efforts to find witnesses in the less-than-cheerful eatery drew a definite dud. Every question they asked of the staff attracted a negative response, and the customer with the crazy eyes slipped out the second they went by him.

G reenwood returned from court and joined Hanson in rifling through the life of Brian Johnson, AKA Sniper, up until the time of his demise. Regarding criminal history and lifestyle, a couple of similarities popped up between him and Davidson. Both were reputed career criminals. While Davidson was mostly known for robberies and drug-related crimes, Johnson reveled in a life of carnage. His track record read almost exclusively of violence, ranging from serious wounding to multiple shootings and murder. Both men were recently released from County Lockup on bond, Davidson on Saturday followed by Johnson on Sunday. No wonder the detectives had begun pondering whether the men fingered something inside County Lockup that got them killed. That perhaps they stepped on the wrong toes or stumbled on something they shouldn't have.

"Okay. McBride, you and Cruikshank get over to County and dig into their movements while in custody. Lean on anyone they bunked with. Interview everyone they interacted with there. What about Johnson's next of kin? Find out from Hanson who he lived with at Powell Ave?" Alyssa instructed.

Toombs got on the phone for a couple of minutes then spoke to Payne. "Hanson thinks Johnson lived with his girlfriend Daniela Scott. The lease is in her name."

"Alright, Toombs, let's go hear what the girlfriend has to say about her man. Hopefully, she will shed some light on who dropped the hammer on him," Alyssa said.

Not a lot was said between them during the fifteen minutes' drive to Johnson's residence. They took US 40 to Powell Avenue. An old gray-haired lady watched from the half-drawn curtain of her second-floor window. A fellow dressed in a checkered shirt made haste as he slipped away from the ice cooler and cut the detectives off before they made it to Johnson's apartment. When he spoke, his voice was soft and low, like a half whisper.

"I heard what happened to Sniper. That somebody finally cut that viper down. So, is it true, is the son of a bitch really dead?" the man asked.

"That's very compassionate of you. Why all the kind words?" Toombs replied.

"I'll tell you why I'm glad that free loader is gone. This place might not seem like much to a hotshot like you, but it's mine. A year ago, I leased the apartment to a young woman named Daniela Scott, a real sweetheart and a hottie too. Two months later, she took up with that lowlife Sniper. With a street name like that, he was rotten goods, and she should have known better," the sleepy guy said.

"Where is Daniela now. Is she at the apartment?" Toombs said.

"I haven't seen her in eight months. She ran off and left that worthless criminal in the apartment. I haven't collected a single dime since she vanished. Sniper said the only thing I would collect is a bullet if I went to the authorities. He laughed in my face, walked around like he owned the damn place. So, damn right I'm glad he's dead."

"Can you let us in? We need to take a look around."

"Be glad to. I've waited long enough to see the back of that rotten skunk. It's on the second floor, I'll take you to it."

He gave his name as Jacob Dunn and led the way to apartment 13 on the second floor. The huge bunch of keys dangled from his waistband and jiggled noisily with every step he took. He opened the door and attempted to enter, but Alyssa stopped him and made it clear they would take it from there. A shotgun was found in a closet and two small bags of smack on the table. A copy of Johnson's bail bond was also on the table under an overflowing ashtray. He was bailed out by Pope's Bail Bond and the surety was Vincent Goudy. Alyssa studied the paper with acute interest.

"The name Goudy is turning into a major magnet for murders, isn't he? This is the second time the name surfaced in as many murders. That, my friend, has bought him a sit-down with Columbus's finest," Alyssa said.

"I couldn't agree more. Let's look into his life a little before extending the invite. You never know, he may have something worth seeing," Toombs replied.

Chapter Four

Daniel peered across the table at Alyssa as they sat down with two cold glasses. The mesmeric melodies from B.B. King's "The Thrill is Gone" softly swirled in the background. The mystery in his eyes made it clear he had questions on his mind. Just not the kind of questions they were accustomed to navigating. Whatever it was, it seemed to have been marinating deep in his mind for quite some time. A rare moment of obvious awkwardness between the duo who held no punches splitting it down the middle.

"So, any chance I'll meet my grandkids before they plant my headstone in the ground? You can't keep turning down all your potential husbands, you know," Daniel said.

"Really, Dad? Where did that come from?"

"Are you saying that question never crossed your mind even once? There's gotta be more than work in your life. What about love? You need someone to make you smile sometimes. It shouldn't only be about the job," Daniel said, swallowing a drink of his bourbon.

"You aren't holding any punches tonight, are you? The truth is, my plate is full right now. I don't know if I could juggle a serious relationship and the job at the same time. When the time comes, I'll handle it, but until then, the job will have to do for now," Alyssa said.

Having clarified her stance on the issue, their conversation returned to more comfortable topics. Regardless of the more palatable shift, it didn't take long before Alyssa bid him good night and turned in. Daniel stewed on the unlikely chance he would be meeting grandkids any time soon and massaged his beard with his fingers. If nothing else, he understood Alyssa well enough to know that no amount of prodding would bring fruit until she was good and ready. So, he drained his glass and called it a night as well.

Much like the day before, the freshness of a brand-new morning brought promises and hope for all things good. Those regarded as wise recognized early on how fragile the line can be. That obscured line between perception and reality never failed to test the tenacity of the detectives who worked at homicide.

No one knew better that those appearances frequently featured fantastic capacity for deception and willful distractions. In a city like Columbus that had witnessed its fair share of heartless men mesmerized by murder, an open mind was always a safer bet than blissful blindness.

Alyssa ventured outdoors to the quietness of the new day, save for the lively song sparrow that came calling with enthusiasm. Daniel was out of sight grooming the horses in the stables.

The long-established notion that most Wednesdays seemed like quite a heavy lift to many remained true, but not to Alyssa. There never seemed to be the need for motivation where she was concerned. So, she checked her Glock and headed off to work like always. Replays of the murders penetrated her brain, and she took it for a deep dive into overdrive. The murder books read tragedy from beginning to end, and so too did the evidence board. They presented a unique set of circumstances that forecasted challenging times for homicide. Career criminals bludgeoned to death and dumped along the city streets was not a good sign for anyone. What message was this daring killer or killers trying to send?

McBride and Cruikshank's visit to the county lockup did little to bring them closer in identifying a likely mastermind within the walls. Nothing that even narrowly resembled a motive for the men's murder was uncovered during their short stint in the facility. Several hours of camera footage were reviewed and multiple inmates and staff interviewed. Yet, no credible evidence was ferreted out connecting anyone there to the killings. As logical a theory as it was, no supporting facts kept it alive. At least, not at the moment.

Davidson's cellmate told the detectives that before Davidson bonded out, he spoke a lot about making major lifestyle changes. Said he found God and dropped a whole mouth full about laying off the crime for the straight and narrow. While the claim may have surprised his criminal associates, it didn't quite rise to a motive for murder.

Telephone conversations were thoroughly screened and scrutinized, but the detectives couldn't find anything in the sometimes-coded chatter that landed them an actionable lead. Apart from a slight skirmish between Johnson and another arrestee in the over a sandwich, there was nothing else of note to report.

Alyssa settled into a few seconds of silence while the briefing sank in.

"Are you both satisfied with what you found there, or should I say what you didn't find? I mean, are you comfortable that the hit didn't originate inside those walls?" Alyssa asked.

"Nothing we learned there suggested that level of organization. Moreover, Johnson was held in lockdown the entire time due to his violent confrontation. That means his ability to communicate freely with others was curtailed to the point of near impossibility," Cruikshank said.

"In Davidson's case, he spent two weeks in jail. He spent his time in housing unit 2, which is a completely different housing unit from where Johnson was confined. As far as we can tell, there was no interaction between Johnson and Davidson. Outside of an elaborate conspiracy by officials at the jail to conceal information, I feel confident what we found is accurate. We saw no evidence to suggest anything questionable at that scope," McBride said.

A peek into the background of Pastor Vincent Goudy painted a perfect picture of the saintly man of the cloth. The charismatic preacher made his debut on the public stage in 2013 when he appeared and started to echo the community's cries. Later the same year, he opened the Guiding Light Tabernacle in Franklinton. Since then, he'd carved out quite a name for himself, fighting for the and forgotten. Many looked to his church as a place of refuge, and to him as a voice of reason and wisdom. His steady rise in popularity showed no sign of slowing down. The church expanded at the rear to accommodate a boxing gym where he coached at-risk youths from the community who had lost their way. Goudy also assisted vulnerable families with bonding their love ones out of jail amidst his groundswell of congregants who lauded him and supported his efforts.

"So, where is the dirt on him? In this day and age, nobody is that noble and untainted. Where was this messiah before 2013, and what was he doing then?" Alyssa asked.

"Couldn't find anything on him until he showed up hooting and hollering on behalf of the disadvantage. So far, he seems to be as clean as a whistle," Hanson replied.

"Okay. See what you can find on Daniela Scott's whereabouts. We need to know why she ran away from her apartment leaving everything behind. Whatever her reason, we need to be sure it wasn't a strong enough motive for murder."

"I'll get right on it," Hanson said.

"Hey, Toombs, I think it's time we pay a visit to our local messiah," Alyssa said.

"You bet, partner. No one knows more about what goes on in these streets than these village leaders. Regardless, what he decides to share with us is left to be seen," Toombs said, then slid his jacket over his shoulders.

T he Guiding Light Tabernacle sat on a one-acre lot at a cul-de-sac in Franklinton. Beautiful palms spaciously spanned the perimeter, their outstretched limbs swaying above faded benches. The church building seemed ancient with its century-old design that hung like the last of the dinosaurs. The double doors at the rear opened onto the courtyard, which led to the more recently constructed gymnasium.

Alyssa and Toombs entered the church from the front. A lonely flag flapped noisily from the pole that hoisted it high in the air. Towering doors opened with handles expertly fashioned to give the illusion of placing one's hand inside the holy bible. Inside, well-polished benches lined both sides of the aisles front to back. Halfway down the passageway, they were greeted with kind words and outstretched arms from the stone-face Goudy.

"God's richest blessings to the officers of the law. Welcome to the temple of the Lord," the penitent preacher said.

"Thanks for taking the time," Payne said.

Quick firm handshakes and brief introductions preceded the short walk by a lonely water fountain out back through the courtyard. Though the pastor was relatively slim, he was muscle-bound like a boxer in his prime. If nothing else worked in the gym, his transformation was a mammoth success story. Something about this mysterious preacher made Alyssa shiver. The kind of frightening façade that's easy to detect, yet difficult to accurately decipher.

"Apart from your regular Sunday service, what is it that you actually do here? From what I observed, you offer a lot more than words of spiritual encouragement to your congregants."

"Indeed, we do. Where I come from, words without deeds are as good as dead. That's why our number one mission here is to transform the lives of those most vulnerable, those most susceptible to a life of crime. Those willing to make sacrifices and work hard will realize meaningful changes. Those who understand that it's by the sweat of their brows they will eat bread."

"So, in a practical sense, how do you accomplish such an ambitious undertaking? I'm pretty sure many of your clients already have issues with the law."

"That's absolutely right. That's why we found real-life solutions to steer them back on the path of righteousness. A chance to build instead of tearing down. Walk with me and witness for yourself the powerful progress at play."

Goudy pointed across the courtyard to a group of people seated around tables. Their attention seemed fully focused on the smartly dressed woman who wrote on a board and instructed them. Bar charts and colorful graphs formed parts of her presentation, and they seemed to be soaking up every bit of what she fed them.

"That right there is a teacher from the community college volunteering her invaluable expertise to our efforts. Trying to steer those fallen off the wagon back on track. Missing a step or two doesn't necessarily mean there isn't another path. She's giving them what they need to know about starting and operating a small business. Business plan and all," Goudy said.

"That's empowering."

Goudy entered the gym with a proud lift in his pitch. "This here is where we try to tame the raging monster roaring within these youngins. Many of them are straddling on the cusp of disaster. Teach them discipline and restraint. You know, show them to exhale in a lawful manner."

Toombs looked around the nicely decorated gym. "Taming the tiger within, are you? It's certainly an admirable effort you're making here, helping the community in such a selfless way."

Goudy smiled for the first time. "God is good. He's always ready to aid those who want to be helped."

"Your name came up twice in our investigation into two recent murders. Brian Johnson and Fabian Davidson. How well did you know them before you bonded them out?" Payne asked.

"My knowledge of those two men is as wobbly as a worn-out wagon wheel. I knew them only because we run a program that helps many of meager means to bond their loved ones out of county. Parents and grandparents come to our church in their worst hours of despair. Detective, we do what we can to ease their distress, nothing more, nothing less."

"Did you know them personally?"

"I meet and greet people every day. Doesn't mean I know anything about who they are or what they do. The gym is quite popular with many of our young men. Is it possible they may have visited from time to time? Absolutely."

Payne's unease with the preacher's response ached for a reciprocal reaction, but she knew too well that would yield nothing useful. She glanced at Toombs, who turned to face her.

"Unfortunately, murder is an occupational hazard for those who choose crime as a career. Even so, we intend to find the perpetrator and bring him to justice," Toombs said.

"I know the relationship between your department and some folks hasn't always been smooth, but I have faith. The community is nervous about the killings and though I do what I can to reassure them, they fear some kind of turf war is fixing to flame."

"Can you tell us anything about why you think these men are dead? Anyone you could point us to who might know?" Payne said.

"I'm afraid not. If you leave your card, I'll ask around and reach out if I learn anything."

Goudy's forthrightness made it perfectly clear he had nothing further he wanted to share with the detectives.

Payne saw no benefit in pushing at that point, and they took their leave. Though her nature was to be skeptical, at times she wondered whether she was being excessively critical. She entertained the possibility she was leaning too stridently on the notion Goudy had skeletons in his closet. He might very well turn out to be a noble man with good intensions for the community. Apart from the fact that Goudy's name appeared on the bail bonds for the two victims, nothing suggested he'd done anything wrong. That meant they had nothing on the board in terms of suspects. Nothing thus far pointed them in the direction of anyone.

CHAPTER FIVE

Payne and her partner hovered over the evidence boards, sniffing for anything they might have missed. Unfortunately, it didn't take long before their study was cut short. Cruikshank drew their attention to the fact that his partner, Detective McBride, didn't turn up for work and couldn't be reached by telephone. Some close to him might say he seemed somewhat out of sorts lately. McBride was allowed some flexibility given the gravity of loss he'd suffered over the preceding months.

Witnessing the suicide of his former mentor, Detective Nelson, would certainly haunt him for a long time to come. As part of the administrative process, McBride and the rest of the team were evaluated and officially cleared for duty by the department's psychiatrist. No one knew the reason for his no-show, but those known facts were top of mind for the people close to him. Their level of concern was understandably elevated since going dark was out of character for him. Still, no one had reason to believe anything grave had happened to him.

Without hesitation, Detective Cruikshank volunteered to swing by McBride's apartment and report back. Payne told Cruikshank to call her when he got there. She then informed Toombs they were going for a drive. Doctor Sherman had bumped up Johnson's autopsy two hours early. That was sweet music to Payne's ears. Anything that had potential to provide valuable information in the case was welcome news. When they arrived, Doctor Sherman awaited them, hovering over Johnson's body, which was face up on a table. He glanced over his glasses at the approaching detectives and smiled.

"Aw. Detectives, right on time."

"Hey, Doc. I have to say it looks a little like you're interrogating the stiff. Did he say anything you'd like to share?" Payne asked.

"Guess I was, wasn't I? Actually, Mr. Johnson here had quite a bit to say."

"Well, I'm just dying to hear whatever he coughed up." Toombs slipped into a paper gown and a pair of XL gloves.

"I think I'll first have a look at his interior before sharing his message."

Payne was somewhat taken aback by Sherman's rare moment of reticence. He hardly ever skipped an opportunity to share his opinion with anyone with a listening ear. This gave her hope that the good doctor was on to something promising. As the procedure got underway, Sherman had no hesitation talking into the microphone. He hovered over the decedent from head to toe with a magnifying glass. Then Sherman paused the recorder and called Payne closer to the table.

"I recalled you saying something about the deceased telling us where he'd been. Well, he hasn't yet said exactly where, but I think he's trying to say what happened to him."

"What did you find?" Payne asked.

"Take a look here. This watermark is far too much for tears. I also noticed the same thing with Davidson, so I went back and looked at him. Someone doused them with some kind of liquid. I've already collected samples. There's plenty on their clothes. The guys at your crime lab should have more to tell," Sherman said.

"Good catch. I'll get the clothes to Julius at the lab. I am hoping their shoes might have tracked something from where they were killed. So, is there any indication what the liquid is?"

"Actually, I ran a preliminary examination of the substance on the decedents. It didn't appear to contain anything toxic or corrosive. It seemed to be water. I expect a deeper study in the laboratory will give a more precise perspective. I'll say this: from the watermarks on the clothing, the upper bodies got the most of it," Sherman said.

"Could be the killer's body fluid," Toombs said.

"No. The killer didn't pee on them, if that's what you're implying. In terms of trauma, the poor fellow got the hard end of a blunt object. Massive bruising of the tissues. Quite similar to Davidson, he suffered multiple fractures. Thirteen broken ribs. The right and left arms had multiple fractures to the ulna, radius, and humerus. See here, the cranium collapsed from two deadly blows. The femurs and left fibula are completely shattered here and here. Left middle and fore fingers fractured at the metacarpal and phalanges. The right clavicle is completely separated with one massive blow. The poor fellow was violently disassembled. Several of the blows must have been administered postmortem. I went over the bodies with a magnifying glass, looking for splinters from the weapon, but found nothing."

"You don't believe the weapon is made of wood. You think it's most likely made of metal," Payne said.

"I do. With this level of damage, a wooden object would likely leave splinters behind. Some tiny components of its construct."

"The similarities are far too overwhelming to ignore. Same weapon. Same killer or killers. What the fuck is his motivation? Why is he so personally inspired for violence?" Toombs said.

Payne and Toombs argued the case on the way back to the homicide office, digging for a perspective that aligned with the evidence they'd gathered. At the very least, they both acknowledged the likelihood that a physically agile killer wielding an iron pipe was hunting in the city streets. The homicides didn't appear any at all random. The million-dollar question was who was behind the killings? Why decimate these troubled men with such brutal extremity? Why punish their loved ones with the knowledge of how gravely they suffered? Numerous questions swirled in Alyssa's head, but the vibration of her phone wrestled her attention away. Cruikshank was calling.

"I found him. It might be a good idea to swing by and see for yourself."

"Is it bad?" Payne asked.

"It's not good."

"Alright, stay close. On my way."

Without saying a word to Toombs, Payne swung the vehicle around, edging the soft shoulder as the vehicle turned, sending Toombs slamming against the door. He mumbled something about not getting a heads-up, but Alyssa was numb to his whiny reaction. She kept her head down, swallowing distance like she was hungry for the road. Toombs thought she was more than a little intense, but he also knew the urgency was necessary and justified. Putting her thumb on the scale to ensure the safety of a colleague really gave no cause for hesitation. Not with Alyssa.

When they arrived, Cruikshank's car was parked behind McBride's along the street in front of the house. The headlight on McBride's car was smashed, including the front grill and bumper, but there was no sign of broken glass on the ground. Whatever happened to the car must have taken place somewhere else. Alyssa looked at the damage then stared at Toombs. It was one of those stares that required no words to impart its probing purview. They went silently through the waist-high foliage to the front door. Toombs raised his hand to knock, but Cruikshank opened the door before he could. From the smirk on

Cruikshank's face, he must have found it funny that Toombs' hand was left dangling in the air like a fallen leaf.

Payne gazed at McBride, still donning her querying expression. "Detective, what have we here? You had us worried sick going off the grid like that."

McBride dropped his head a bit. "That's all on me. There's no justifiable excuse I could give for my poor judgment. I should have called."

"So, what's up with the car and your arm in a sling? You look like hell on wheels ran you over. Who is your beautiful guest? Aren't you going to introduce us?"

"Absolutely. This is Fay. She lost control of her car and slammed head on into me on Seventh Avenue last night. Her car is a lot worse than mine. Fortunately, she came out without a scratch. The doctor said my shoulder was dislocated and popped it back into place."

"And you brought her home with you?"

"Just until her car is sorted out. She's sticking around a little while until some obstacles are figured out."

Sensing the awkwardness in the sitting room, Toombs requested water from Fay and followed her into the kitchen. Apart from appearing a touch shy, Fay was quite the head-turner. Relatively tall and perky with gorgeous hair. She was smoking hot. As easy as she was on the eyes, the main concern for Alyssa was McBride's state of mind. That was the case before his recent incident and perhaps even more so now. From the look of things, emotionally, it was probably not trending in the best direction. The second Toombs and Fay left the room, Payne positioned herself next to McBride on the couch.

"What the fuck is going on with you, brother? A stranger crashed into you, so do you bring her home? What's up with that?"

"Technically, she's not a stranger. We knew each other back in high school before they moved away. She's struggling right now. Down on her luck, if you know what I mean? I'm just giving a helping hand to someone in need. That's all."

"I hope you know what you're doing with this woman. How long will you be out for?"

"Today and tomorrow until the soreness dissipates. I'll be back in the office on Monday if that's okay with you?"

"I just need to know you're alright. Call if you need anything. Anything at all." She turned away as Toombs came back into the room. "Toombs, what took you so long? Did you boil the water, too?"

"Turned out I was a lot thirstier than I initially thought. I'm ready when you are." He winked at Mack. "Take care, Mack. Holler if you need me."

Cruikshank said his goodbyes as well and walked out, scratching his head like he had a bad case of dandruff. Though Payne thought McBride's situation was more than a little troubling, the second she got to the car, she broke out laughing. She laughed so hard she fell into a coughing spell. The whole scenario sounded so bizarre she really had no clue what to make of it. From Toombs' perspective, McBride had been broadsided by the woman he brought home. The glaring irony may have drawn temporary laughter, but the underlying feeling was one of melancholy.

Payne made the call to Julius about the samples heading his way at the crime lab. The killings demonstrated an unmistakable pattern of deliberate brutality. Still, regarding who was responsible and the motive for the murder, they had nothing tangible to work with. Getting a solid from the lab in any of those areas would mark a pivotal point in the direction of the investigation. Something sufficiently valuable could determine the trajectory forward.

Alyssa considered one significant possibility they hadn't sufficiently explored. She understood perfectly well that not knowing of a witness to any of the murders shouldn't conclude that none existed. If a witness did indeed exist, it would be their job to find them.

D aniel had steaks on the grill and a touch of his favorite bourbon in his glass when Alyssa arrived at the ranch. Nothing beat the ranch for beauty when darkness fell, and lights lit the landscape. The intoxicating melody from John Mayhall and the Bluesbreaker's "So Many Roads" simmered softly in the background.

Life was great for Daniel and Alyssa's father-daughter relationship. He could also read her like a book when it came to deciphering when a case was getting under her skin. Alyssa must have been hungry, because she joined right in with a glass of her own. Minutes later they were knifing their way through a couple of the flame-kissed steaks. Retirement afforded Daniel ample time to master his cooking skills, and he turned every meal into culinary masterpieces.

"This is really good, Dad."

"Probably won't be long until I get fat and croak around the table."

"What?"

"Well, I have plenty of time to cook and even more time to eat."

"But you also have the ranch to run. That's a lot of work for a man who is retired."

"So, how's this big case shaping up? Any luck finding the killer yet?"

"No. This perp is careful and clean. He leaves nothing behind but broken bodies. Nothing that leads back to him. At least, not yet anyway."

"What can I do? I can poke around my old playgrounds if you like?"

"Not that anything I say will stop you anyway. This killer is really brutal, so I need you to stay away from this one."

"I'm enjoying retirement just fine. I do not need to get back in the game or interfere with your work. That doesn't mean I can't ask a question or two of my old friends."

"Okay, Dad. I think I know when it's time to quit an argument with you. Whatever you do, please be careful. That's it for me, I'm about to hit the sack. Love you."

Chapter Six

The Friday morning feel fitted Alyssa in a turtle-neck, above-knee overcoat, and brown leather gloves. Once again, McBride was noticeably absent from the morning briefing. It was no oversight that very little detail was revealed about his unavailability for duty. Alyssa just said he'd taken a couple of days to take care of pressing personal issues. She believed the rest was up to McBride. He could share with the others if he desired to do so. Until his issues became a problem that endangered him or others, his privacy would be left up to him to disseminate at his own pleasure.

Payne drew their attention to the evidence board while she zeroed in on the details of the case. She identified a few unresolved areas for immediate focus. The first thing she mentioned was that they were still in search of the primary crime scenes in both murders. Which meant the men were killed elsewhere and transported to the dump sites. Payne wanted to know what type of vehicle was used to transport the bodies and how the killer accomplished the drops without being noticed?

"This is how it's going to go. Hanson and Greenwood, neither of you visited any of the crime scenes. I need fresh eyes on them. Go to Davidson's dump scene, then Johnson's. Compare everything that seems out of place for similarities. If cameras exist, find them. Look for any possibility of a witness."

"We'll get right on it," Hanson said.

"Cruikshank, check with control and see if anyone called in suspicious activities near the crime scenes. In fact, anywhere in the city between 8 p.m. and 5 a.m. on the nights of the murders. Also, review street cams leading to the scenes for a possible transport vehicle. Any vehicle appearing near both scenes must be viewed as highly suspicious."

"Sure thing," Cruikshank said.

"Toombs, we still need to find Daniela Scott to hear what she has to say about her man. Track her down. She can't be that difficult to find. Buzz me when you have an address."

"Standby. Hit you back shortly."

"Alright, ladies. That's all for now. Get off your asses and go find us some evidence," Payne said, waving their departure with both hands.

Lieutenant Lorrigan wanted an update from Payne on the murders. He hinted that the pressure from above was much less when the victims were career criminals. Nevertheless, murder is murder regardless of where they were committed or who was killed. The communities of concern were not decorated with magnificent mansions and manicured lawns outlined with palms. Consequently, residents tended to feel they had little or no access to their public representatives. They certainly wouldn't be sipping cocktails next to them at country clubs and banquets. It was probably no surprise they were so susceptible to the loudest voices that claimed to represent their interest. Voices such as Pastor Goudy and others like him. The so-called local savior of the people and man of the cloth. These communities were natural powder kegs waiting to explode onto the streets, and Lorrigan knew it. As far as he was concerned, crimes in any form were bad for the city and must be stopped and the perpetrators caught and put away. He needed this killer behind bars. He needed this brutal killer caught sooner rather than later.

Payne heard Lorrigan's message loud and clear, and it was no different from her stance on the issue. This brutal killer must be caught, extracted from the city streets, and swiftly brought to justice. Citizens were confident in the CPD's ability to maintain law and order. Still, those favorable realities were not sufficient to sway Lorrigan or Payne into complacency. They knew how difficult it was to build trust on the streets. They also understood how easily that trust could be eroded and burned to the ground.

Commendable as it was, their monumental accomplishment was fragile and intangible. It had to be nurtured and maintained with constant work like combing one's hair or brushing one's teeth every morning. That was the key to Payne being so proficient at her job. She never stopped working to extricate the streets from their most violent murderers to maintain the safety of the city and its citizens.

"Bingo. You can run, but you can't hide," Toombs shouted. "Payne, I found her."

"Where?"

"I don't have her home address yet, but she works at a coffee shop on Grant Avenue. I made a call, and she's on the job right now. We can probably get there in thirty, depending on traffic."

"Okay. Let's hear what this fleeing damsel has to say for herself. If what her landlord said is true, she probably had reason enough to want Sniper dead."

"If a women's scorn can break a man's bones in so many places, please remind me never to piss you off."

B y the time they pulled away from Marconi Boulevard, the sun was fighting through the sleepy clouds. The constant rivalry between the two made it almost impossible to declare a clear winner. This unending struggle between the darker shades of the day and sunny skies, in many ways, reflected the madness of men on display. The same madness that left those two men with broken bones and hearts that no longer beat. Traffic was light as they left the homicide office behind and slipped onto King Avenue.

The hope was that Daniela Scott would shed a little light on anything in the lifestyle of her former lover that may have led to his death. Spouses are often the first suspects investigators look at in their search for perpetrators in crimes such as this one. However, something peculiar about these murders already had Payne's crew cocking their eyes in other directions. Nevertheless, everyone had to be thoroughly examined and cleared for the investigative process to take its course.

The name tag on her shirt said *Daniela*. Toombs took one look and concurred what Daniela's landlord said about her being a hottie. Payne seated herself near the rear in the cafeteria. Away from the five people enjoying various flavors of hot beverages. Not only was the warmth inside pleasant but the aroma was enticing. Payne watched Daniela's reaction as Toombs approached her and spoke with her briefly. Toombs then joined Payne at the table while Daniela finished serving an elderly couple chatting her ear off.

"Detectives, I don't mean to be rude, but this is my job. What can I do for you?" Daniela said.

"We won't be long. We have a few questions about Fabian Davidson. Sniper," Payne said.

"What about him? I want nothing to do with that monster. I wish to God I never heard that name ever again."

"I understand you were involved in a relationship. What happened?"

"Did he send you here? Does he know I work here? I'm sorry, I have to go now."

"Daniela, stop. Sniper is dead," Toombs said.

"What? Dead?"

"You heard right. He's gone for good. He was murdered two nights ago. Do you know anything about that?" Toombs asked.

"You can't be serious. Where were you when he almost strangled me to death? I didn't see any detective then. Now that someone finally stood up to him, you're looking at me?"

"We're not accusing you of anything. We're here because we believe you might be able to help us find his killer," Payne said.

"My help? How can I help you when I haven't seen or spoken to Sniper in months? I ran away from my apartment to escape from him. Honestly, I don't see any way I could be of help to you."

"Sometimes it's the little things you don't take notice of that solve the puzzle. We just need you to answer a few questions."

"I left my apartment eight months ago. Changed my phone number so he couldn't contact me. I left everything I owned back there when I realized how dangerous he was. Since then, I've stayed with friends and worked at this shop. This little coffee shop saved me. I haven't seen or heard from Sniper since leaving."

"Lucky for you, your stuff is still at the apartment. You can go back home now. He can't hurt you anymore," Toombs said.

"Do you know anyone who wanted him dead? Who do you think killed him?" Payne said.

"I don't know. I feared him. Everything about him frightened me. At times, I wished him gone for good. Now that he's gone, I'm happy I don't have to look over my shoulder all the time. Still, I swear to you; I have no idea who killed him."

T he journey back to the office seemed more pleasant than the earlier run out. The sun finally overpowered the clouds with its sprawling yellow glow. Traffic was a lot lighter. The thing that remained the same was that they were no closer to catching the killer now than before. The investigation certainly wasn't shaking fast enough in the direction they would have liked. However, most seasoned detectives made peace with the fact that the tedious road to triumphant prosecutions and convictions takes time. Particularly, in complicated cases where perpetrators exhibit proficiency with planning and premeditation of their crimes. No one understood better than Alyssa Payne that there was no such thing as a perfect crime. What it required was personnel with the right aptitudes and perseverance to pursue the cases and prove it.

As Toombs pulled the truck into the driveway, Payne took a call from Julius. He confirmed Doctor Sherman's preliminary findings. The liquid substance found on the upper bodies and clothes of both decedents was indeed regular tap water. The water was consistent with that distributed throughout the city for regular domestic consumption. Nothing in the results suggested any other chemical solution was added, nor was anything extracted. It was water that could have been collected from any faucet within the city. Though the chemical analysis found nothing peculiar about the water, it opened a range of questions about the killer. Questions that were already twisting and turning inside Payne's brain.

"What the devil is this killer doing? Why is it that the weird ones always choose to commit murders here in Columbus?" Payne said.

"What's that about, partner?"

"That was Julius. The liquid on our decedents is water like Sherman said. What if the perp is cleansing them in some way?"

"Why would he clean them before dumping them like roadkill?"

"You can ask him when we catch him. We keep a tight lid on the liquid. Not a breath of it goes out to the public. Hopefully, he doesn't realize we picked up on it. You never know, he might just let something else slip next time."

"Next time? You think there will be more bodies, don't you?"

"This evil bastard is too motivated to quit now. He's having too much fun to walk away. Yes, unfortunately, there will be more bodies."

T he office was partially empty and quiet with Hanson and Greenwood out in the field. Cruikshank was flying solo until McBride returned off leave. He was busy reviewing call logs and camera feed. During his persistent perusal of the records, Cruikshank stumbled on a call made on the emergency line on Sunday January 2 at 10:10 p.m. the same night Davidson was murdered. The call was made from an unregistered number and lasted only a few seconds.

The female caller sounded terrified. "Send help. They're killing him. Hurry, Franklinton Park."

The operator sent out patrols but nothing out of the ordinary was observed. There were approximately twelve parks within the Franklinton area, and the call didn't specify which one. That created quite a challenge for patrol, resulting in longer response times in several cases. Eventually, the officers reported no unusual activities. As for the camera feed, no vehicle was spotted at or near both murder scenes up to that time. Several hours of footage remained to be reviewed, though Cruikshank was watching it at a heightened speed. Reviewing all that footage in real-time would require too many hours.

Payne was in a less-than-cheerful mood after learning that a potential witness to Davidson's killing was in the wind. The caller was imprecise on the location of the incident but the sound of vehicles going by was unmistakable in the background. Franklinton had too many parks, and the call ended before the operator could ask which park it was. That lack of information may have contributed to the patrol's inability to locate either the caller or the incident.

Toombs suggested the caller may have been a stranger passing through. If she was from the area, she would have known there were other parks in Franklinton. Payne believed there was logic to Toombs' reasoning unless the tip was called in as a decoy to the actual event. The call could have been made as a deliberate distraction to divert officers from the scene of the action. Whatever it was, Payne was not about to let it slide. She instructed Cruikshank to continue reviewing street cam feeds to include cameras near the parks.

Hanson and Greenwood returned from their visit to the dump sites. They discovered two small pools of motor oil within ten feet of both bodies. In each case, the pool only had about three or four drops of oil. That suggested whatever vehicle was parked there probably wasn't parked for long and wasn't leaking very fast. Hanson said the crime scene personnel had collected samples and taken photographs. If nothing else, this new discovery supported the evidence that the same perpetrator was involved in both killings. It was also an indication that the same vehicle was used to transport both bodies. That also gave the team one more thing to look for when they located the vehicle. It most likely would have an oil leak.

"With all these similarities simmering to the surface, I find gaping conflicts in the murderer's methods. Bear with me a minute, will you? The first body was dumped at a lonely dead-end road like he wanted to conceal it. On the other hand, the second body was dumped on the city street for all to see. Why take six of Davidson's fingers while Johnson had all ten of his still intact? To me, that kind of contrast is quite telling," Payne said.

"Could be he's transitioning really fast. Learning and liking the thrills of the kill more as he goes along," Toombs said.

"Could be, but this is how I view it. Either he has personality issues, or he's not working alone. We might have a deadly team on our hands here. Each with his own individual taste for brutality. Imagine this for a second. Two or more murderers working together. Each unleashing his own unique brand of brutality. If this hypothesis is even close to correct, we need to bring them down before their teamwork improves. Before they start killing in synergy," Payne said.

CHAPTER SEVEN

Night swept in swiftly and swallowed the city within its starless solar shadow. Noisy crickets cried their tiny hearts out like madmen with megaphones. A huge owl hooted midflight as it started its hunt for a nightcap. Alyssa leaned against the railing at the ranch, gazing down at the landscape. She moistened her lips with a sip from the iceless bourbon in her glass. She gazed about and realized Daniel's truck was gone from its usual parking spot. That was no cause for alarm; she presumed he was probably out somewhere having a cold one. Moments later, she drained her glass, grabbed a street map of the city, and headed up the magnificent staircase.

Alyssa awoke early Saturday morning with an ambitious mission in mind. So, she made a call and rallied the troops. The full team was not expected in the office that morning, but the significance of Alyssa's plan took precedence. Alyssa was the first one to arrive. Then, within a few minutes, they all trickled in behind her. Toombs arrived with a tray of coffee, which he passed around like a church communion. Once they were all there, Payne pulled up a map of the city on the computer. She huddled them closer together and centered their attention to the map on screen.

"Those of you who weren't supposed to be here this morning, thanks for coming in. Toombs said something yesterday that kept bugging me all night. You said the caller might be from out of town and didn't know there were other parks in Franklinton. Now, that got me thinking: what if you were right?" Payne asked.

"If I was, it could be any of those twelve parks," Toombs said.

Those parks are open every day. The scene would likely be trampled and corrupted by visitors," Greenwood said.

"Even if the scene was tarnished, it would still be significant to know where Davidson was actually killed," Hanson said.

"We don't have the manpower to search twelve parks thoroughly. The caller was too vague for us to call in the level of resources necessary to accomplish that task. Upstairs would never go for it," Cruikshank said.

"What do you know? You're all correct. Spot on in your assessments of the circumstances," Payne said.

"So, what are we doing here then?" Toombs said.

"I admit this exercise is a long shot, but this is what we're going to do. It occurred to me that the most centrally located parks were more likely to be identified with Franklinton by the caller. With that in mind, I've selected three parks to focus on this morning. We heard vehicles in the caller's background, which made us think she was on or near the road. We will not attempt to search the entire parks, only the areas near the streets. Areas with a good line of sight from the roadway. Remember, time is not on our side. By 9 a.m., visitors will likely start coming in, and we want to be in and out of there by then."

"You really think this will work?" Greenwood asked.

"I guess we won't know until we try, will we? We'll break into three teams. Each team will have the support of a K9 and two uniforms from patrol. Cruikshank, you're still flying solo without McBride. You'll take Rhode's Park. Hanson and Greenwood, you'll cover Cody Park. Toombs and I will take McKinley Park. The crime scene team will be standing by. If you have questions, now is your chance to ask them," Payne said.

Apparently, no one had questions. If they did, they kept the lid on them. Payne and her team pulled into the entrance at McKinley Park. The K9 handler alighted from his pickup and prepped his four-legged partner for the prowl. Deputy Scott had seven years under his belt. The last five were spent at the K9 Division. His partner for two years was a German shepherd named Toph.

Payne pointed out the general target areas to the search team. Scott gave Toph a good whiff of Davidson's shirt, gave him the command to go, and turned him loose. Payne, Toombs, and the other two patrol deputies diligently scanned the surroundings for anything belonging to Davidson or possible signs of violence.

Payne met with the park manager and requested surveillance footage from the cameras there. The problem with that request was that the cameras only stored recordings for twenty-four hours. Once the hours elapsed, the feed automatically erased. Payne inquired about the staff on duty the night in question.

Though they were not on duty at that time, the manager produced the post takeover log for the night of the murder. According to the brief, the night was incident free with no unusual occurrences to note.

After an hour elapsed, Toph failed to detect a scent. Eventually, Scott extracted him from the search. Payne realized that location was a definite dud, but she knew from the get-go the whole thing was a long shot. To her, a hit-and-miss further fueled the flames to get out there and try again.

She consulted briefly with Toombs then decided it was time to pull stump at 8:45 a.m. Hanson called and updated Payne about their search. The result at Cody Park came up as equally empty as the one at McKinley. Though Payne was hoping to find evidence and hadn't yet, she would have been more disappointed with herself if she didn't at least make an effort to test the validity of the caller's claim. Perhaps there was something in the caller's voice she couldn't ignore? Fact is, Payne never really required a reason to be diligent and deliberate in following leads.

Mere minutes after talking to Hanson, Cruikshank called from Rhodes Park with a big breakthrough. The dog picked up a scent outside the park, which led to a damaged cell phone in an adjacent vacant lot. The phone was believed to be Davidson's. The phone wasn't the only piece of evidence they discovered. Not far away, they also found a severed finger. In part, the news felt like a break in the case, but in other ways, it felt a little like vindication that she wasn't just chasing thin air. Cruikshank advised that crime scene, which was standing by was already activated. With that bit of good news, Payne gazed across at Toombs then darted away to the scene.

"Finally, we're getting somewhere with this fucking creep," Payne said.

"Payne, how do you unravel this stuff so easily?"

"When I figure out the answer to that, you'll be the first to know."

"You want to know what I think?"

"Not really."

"I'm thinking maybe you were a detective somewhere in another life. Now you're back as a detective with all that knowledge and experience."

"Well, I think your imagination is definitely from another life."

"Payne, I'm just messing with you. Everyone knows you're a chip off the old block."

P ayne parked about 100 meters before reaching the other service vehicles. She wanted to see for herself from a distance what the killer saw in that place that made him choose it. She wondered whether he selected that spot for a specific reason or simply as a matter of convenience?

Payne gazed around full circle. She snapped pictures on her mobile as she went along. The cordoned area was a grassy lot outside the boundaries of the park. The vacant lot had a for sale sign planted near the road that read, *For Sale By Owner. Contact C.F. Malcolm for Further Information.* A telephone number was written at the bottom.

By then, Julius had already bagged and tagged the phone and finger for the lab. Payne walked along the roadway adjacent to the vacant lot. She was looking for that familiar pooling of motor oil, and there it was. It was almost directly in front of where the severed finger and phone were found. She stooped over the spot and stared for a while then signaled to Cruikshank and showed it to him.

"You understand what this means, don't you?" Payne asked.

"Yes. I believe I do."

"We now have three locations and a likely timeline. Triangulate the locations and find whatever route they traveled. They must be on camera somewhere. I need to see those sons of bitches. McBride should be back on Monday to help you with this mountain of work."

"I hope you're right about that. I already had a lot of material to cover before this stuff was discovered."

"You talk to McBride? How's he coming along?"

"Not this morning. We had words yesterday. Honestly, he sounded like a few screws were still rattling loose in his head. You know what? Maybe it's best to wait and see how it goes Monday. You'll see for yourself then. You'll have a chance to see what is what when he returns."

The grass where the items were discovered still harbored significant signs of distress. Though they were beginning to straighten out to their original shapes, the displacement indicated what appeared to be a major struggle. Clearly, something violent occurred there. The full extent of which the detectives may never be able to decipher.

Julius indicated his processing of the scene was complete. Payne looked about until her eyes landed on the closest building to the park. The Milky Way Ice Cream Shop was less than a block away. The shop was closed, though staff could be seen through the glass moving around in preparation for the day's opening. Payne made her way to the crime scene vehicle and slapped Julius with a gripping stare as he packed away his equipment.

"You don't need to tell me about putting a rush on it. As soon as I have results, you'll get it," Julius said.

"Okay, good to know. I'm gonna hold you to that," Payne said.

Alyssa's mood was a lot lighter when she rolled into the ranch that afternoon. Though she wasn't known to be particularly moody, a bit of good news could produce a reciprocal reaction in anyone. She seized two bottles of Miller's from the refrigerator and handed one off to Daniel, who was stirring stew on the stove. They raised bottles like beer buddies while "Slightly Hung Over" from Blues Delight simmered softly on the turntable. After a while Daniel joined her in the sitting room, holding two fresh bottles.

"I didn't hear you come in last night. What happened? Did you party until the sun came up?" Alyssa asked.

"You must be talking about the young Daniel of years ago. I got here before eleven, but you were probably out cold by then."

"I probably was. This case isn't making it easy for us at all. Anyway, there's only one option at play. Bite the bullet and push on ahead like always."

"I went sniffing around the Liquor Bird Bar last night. If anyone there knew anything about the murders, they weren't telling. From what I gather, the gangs aren't claiming the hits either. The streets are completely mute on these guys. I'm not ready to give up yet, though. Eventually, they'll talk, so I'll continue to keep an ear to the ground."

"You're right about that. Sooner or later, the streets will start whispering again. Until then, we'll just have to let the evidence do the talking. These are the kind of cases where we can't afford to miss anything. Every bit of detail counts."

"There you go. Speaking like the learned detective you've mellowed into. I never had your smarts this early on in my career. Compared to you, I was as dumb as they come."

"I know what you're doing, and I'm not buying it. That's not what they say about you. They say your shoes are too big for anyone to fill. Not even me."

"Perhaps this is my way of saying how proud I am to witness your smooth progress. Columbus is certainly a safer place these days with you in the saddle."

Alyssa glanced at her vibrating phone on the couch beside her. Her eyebrows lifted as she swept the phone to her ear. It was McBride. The hurt in his voice told her it was a desperate call for help. Within an instant of answering, she suspected his distress was dire. She stepped back into her boots and scooped her keys from the mahogany table next to her. She gazed at Daniel. He instantly reciprocated then nodded in approval as she hustled out the door.

CHAPTER EIGHT

On Monday morning, the office was bursting at the seams with possibilities from the litany of leads being followed. If optimism was indeed a magnet for success like many said, then the team should be well on their way for a win. One could easily tell by the extra pep in their steps and the light in their eyes they were on to something big. At the very least, everyone appeared motivated and ready to meet the moment. McBride was the early bird of the day. He was eventually brought up to speed by Cruikshank, who got his feet wet while reviewing camera feeds. Payne proceeded straight to her office, where she was joined almost immediately by McBride.

"Thanks for swinging by the house on Saturday. I didn't know who else to call," McBride said.

"Any time. Don't ever hesitate to holler if trouble come knocking, or if you simply want to talk. Alright?" Payne said.

"I'd rather no one knew about Fay ripping me off. I already feel like a fool for bringing that swindler into my house. Then she loots the place and cleans me out of five grand. That's not a good look on me, is it?"

"The optics certainly aren't great, but I'm more concerned about you than I am about that stuff. Shit happens all the time. I wouldn't worry too much about it if I were you."

"Thanks a lot for saying that."

"So, are you sure you don't want to report her? She should be punished for taking advantage of you like that. I know you were only trying to help her out."

"No. Let her go. I can see that going sideways in a million different ways. She's a liar and a thief. Who knows what fairy tale she might conjure up if I file charges against her?"

"I know things haven't been easy on you since Nelson died. It has been hard on all of us, but I know how close you were. You need to talk to someone about it. You can't carry that weight around with you forever. You have to find a way to let it go. That grief will rip you apart and eat you up. So, promise me you'll go talk to someone," Payne said, sticking him with a piercing stare.

"I'll talk to the department's shrink I went to last time. I like her. Yeah, she's okay. I promise."

Payne studied McBride long and hard as he exited the office. He had seen better days. Noticing changes in his behavior was always going to be the easy part. The challenge was finding the best way to help without injuring his pride. She hoped he'd follow through on her recommendation to talk with a professional about his struggles before his situation metastasized. For the time being, she planned to keep an eye on him as much as she could. She sucked in a deep breath like she hungered for it and massaged her chin while she watched him disappeared from view.

J ulius called with an update on Davidson's test results. His stomach content determined he ate vanilla ice cream within an hour of his demise. Julius also confirmed that the severed finger from the park did in fact belong to Davidson.

Payne grabbed her notebook from the desk and flipped it open to the page marked with a yellow clip. She read over a few entries she'd previously made in the case. Her thoughts settled in for a moment then she closed the notebook and stepped out on the floor.

Toombs was talking on the phone when she got to his desk. Whatever was going on with the call, he was pretty jacked up about it. Excitement glowed in his eyes like a chubby kid in a cake shop.

"What the heck was that about? You look like you just won the lottery."

"I think I did. Just not the kind of lottery you're thinking of."

"What the hell are you talking about, partner? You need to speak plain English. Not riddles and parables."

"Someone actually wants to publish my book. Unbelievable, isn't it?"

"Your book? I had no idea you could read, let alone write. For some reason, I always believed your vocabulary was confined to two or three words."

Payne joked around with Toombs a bit before landing loads of praises in his lap for his surprise accomplishment. For Toombs, it was a carefully guarded secret. Many around the office knew he liked to read novels, but none knew he also dabbled in ink in his spare time. Before he slipped away into sleep land at night, he always tried to write at least half a paragraph. Perhaps writing was his outlet. His therapy for all the horrible things he had to process at homicide over the years. His unique method of decompression. Taking it all in day after day, then letting it all out in the form of stories on paper.

Like other Monday mornings, especially ones with matters of significance to discuss, Payne pulled the team together. Arising from last Saturday's discovery, they were all occupied circling the breadcrumbs left behind by the killer. Payne's notebook flipped open once again. This time, it only stayed open for a few seconds. She stood in front of the evidence board gazing back at the attentive faces before her.

"What do we know so far in this case? We now believe Davidson was first assaulted near Rhodes Park. One of his severed fingers was recovered there at what we think is the primary crime scene. At this point, five of Davidson's fingers remain unaccounted for. It is undetermined whether the perpetrators kept them or disposed of them. We can't say if Davidson died there on the spot or at some secondary location, but we believe that was where it all started to go downhill for him," Payne said.

"A few drops of motor oil formed a small pool at the scene. A similar observation was made at the dump sites where both Davidson and Johnson's bodies were discovered," Hanson added.

"We're currently working to triangulate the most likely routs between all three points where the motor oil was discovered. This will narrow down the amount of street cam footage we need to scrutinize. The same method is being utilized separately between both crime scenes connected to Davidson. The primary goal here is to identify the vehicle and occupant involved. Now that McBride is back on the job, things should proceed faster," Cruikshank said.

"There were ants on Davidson's mouth and hands, which explains undigested vanilla ice cream in his stomach. I noticed an ice cream shop next to the park. The Milky Way. It's plausible he bought the ice cream there before he was attacked outside," Payne said.

"Greenwood and I can go over there and see if anyone remembers serving him," Hanson said.

"Leave no stone unturned. If there is camera, you know what to do. Hopefully, someone there noticed something suspicious. Let's also not forget there is still one witness out there somewhere that we know of. She could be anywhere and probably scared to death," Payne said.

"We'll get right on it, but as far as the witness goes, there's no telling who or where she is. If she is a tourist, as suspected, she could be miles away," Hanson said.

The team's energy was vibrant, but something in the air didn't sit right. An atmosphere of quiet unease wrapped around Alyssa's mind like a wet blanket and made the morning appear bleak. Though she had absolutely no idea what triggered the eerie mood, she kept her head down and focused on the case at hand. Payne leaned against the above-waist partition of Toombs's cubicle and gazed down at him seated at his desk. She thought of sharing her dreary intuition but couldn't quite find words to do it justice. Alyssa didn't want to come off sounding overly superstitious or creepy. Her entire background demanded 100 percent fact-based evidence supported by practicality and science. This experience wasn't an indication she was climbing on the crazy train. It was simply one of those moments when instinct played unexplained marvels on the mind.

"I'm going to run an errand. Wanna tag along?" Payne asked.

"You asking me to?"

"You coming or not?"

"I got you, partner. So, where are we going?"

Payne and Toombs left homicide without further discussion of the destination. After a while, Payne veered off Marconi Boulevard onto Broad Street.

Toombs used the awkward silence to talk about his upcoming book. He mentioned it was a crime novel he titled *Murder at Midnight*. That was when he realized that he'd never discussed his book with anyone close to him before. He'd never felt excitement for any of it until the good news came that someone was interested in publishing it. That development made his little pet project alive and real. What had started as a silent search for a purpose in his life away from work was fast becoming something he never envisioned.

Payne didn't interrupt him. She just listened and allowed him to talk. He only stopped talking when the vehicle slipped onto Glenwood Avenue.

Enormous trees cast their shadows above the road. The sun was out but not impressively so. Toombs seemed instantly alert and watchful. He finally started to suspect that Payne's errand wouldn't be a social call when she pulled up in front of a flower shop.

The sign said *Fabulous Flowers* and was decorated with beautiful flowers painted in bright colors. The letters were nicely designed and written in fancy fonts. Payne pointed Toombs to the back of the building while she walked to the front door. She entered the shop and saw no one inside, and no flowers either. Regardless of what was written on the signboard, the flower shop was clearly not open for business. The place appeared unused and abandoned. A few seconds later, Toombs called to her and said he held someone. He came in from the back holding Fay by her arm. She'd tried to flee out the back door and landed right in his waiting hands.

"I caught her trying to fly the coop. Man, she sure knows how to move," Toombs said.

"Fay, why were you running? Thought you could get away that easily?" Payne asked.

"Get away? I wasn't running. I saw your gun and thought it was a stickup. I thought I was being robbed. Can't be too careful these days," Fay said.

"That's really cute coming from a low-class swindler like you. I'm not going to beat around the bush with you any further. You know who I am, don't you?"

"You're McBride's friends. You came to see him after the accident."

"Accident, my ass. Let's clear up a few things. You know, so we're on the same page going forward. I looked into your life a little, and this is what I found. Your name at birth was Faith McMaster. By age twenty-four, you'd already racked up five arrests resulting in three convictions for fraud and conspiracy. That's what you do. You're a thief. A slimy grifter without a conscience."

"Hold on a minute. Let me explain."

"Be quiet. I'm not done with you yet. Apparently, things weren't going well for you in Texas. The cops there quickly caught on to your scam. So, you changed your name to Fay Barnes and moved here. To a fresh field of unsuspecting men for you to target. Tell me, did you target McBride? How did you know he was vulnerable? How do you pick them?" Payne asked.

"The whole thing was a big mistake. I didn't know he was a detective at the beginning. I first noticed him at the gas station. I could tell then he was hurting. So, I watched and waited and rammed his car on purpose. He got out of his car, took one look at me, and mistook me for a woman from his past. All I did from there was play along with it."

"His kindness wasn't good enough for you? You couldn't help yourself. You still had to rob him. Where's the money you lifted from his place? Come on. You're nothing but a greedy scavenger. Hand it over," Payne said.

"Please, in my bag. You'll see. It's all there. Please, don't send me back to prison. If I violate my parole, I'll die behind those walls."

Toombs emptied the contents of Fay's bag on the counter. "Take a look at this. There's at least twenty grand here," Toombs said.

"Where did you get the cash?" Payne asked.

Fay hesitated. "I may have sold a few items from McBride's house. Did you know he collected baseball cards? So, what happens to me now that I've told you the truth about everything? It should count for something that I'm giving back all the cash I got for his stuff, shouldn't it?"

"That depends on how badly you want to avoid going back to prison."

"Just say the word and I'll do it."

"There's only one way. Two things you gotta do. First, you take us to wherever you sold the cards. Once we get the cards back, you only have one more thing to do."

"Name it."

"Pick a state. Any state that's not Ohio. Then you get the fuck away from here and away from McBride. You don't call him. Don't write him. You don't even remember his name."

"You don't have to worry. After today, I'm gone for good. I would rather go to hell than back to prison. There's something else you should know about McBride. At times, I thought he knew I wasn't the woman from his past. It's like he didn't care that I was using him," Fay said, sinking into a pensive stare.

The mood was mellow when they drove away from Fay's crooked fencer. Toombs seemed happy and animated, ranting about how badass Payne was by making Fay confess to her grift on McBride. Still, he was unable to resist the opportunity to express his displeasure that Payne hadn't apprised him of the details beforehand. Payne quickly smoothed it over with a calming smile and a switch of the subject.

It was well into the afternoon when they arrived back at homicide. Payne had barely made it to her office when the dreaded call came in. The killer had struck again; he'd dropped another body.

Chapter Nine

When Payne pulled up at the scene, the departing sun appeared ready to relinquish duty to the approaching night. The sky was a rustic orange. A man's body was dramatically staged to slump over the steering wheel of a car. The narrow dirt road ran off West Broad Street across the road from Rhodes Park. It ended at what seemed like a waterless creek in the thick of the woods. Huge trees covered the road and repelled what little brightness remained of daylight from shining through.

The car was a white Accord with an Ohio tag. Toombs pointed to a second set of tire tracks with significantly wider wheels than the Accord. The tracks stopped about five feet behind the Accord then circled back onto the main street. Julius and three men from his CSU team got to work measuring and photographing the tire tracks. They also made casts of the tracks.

Payne gazed up at the fire-red sky then moved toward the body. Cesar Espinosa had been working as Doctor Sherman's assistant for the better part of five years. He was the man on the ground that evening while Sherman was occupied elsewhere with other engagements.

Payne studied the body in silence for a moment. He leaned forward over the steering wheel with his arms resting on his thighs. His eyes were wide open. His head was slightly slanted so he steered off into the orange sunset. This victim had suffered significantly worse head and facial trauma than the previous two. Missing teeth and a dislocated jaw were Espinosa's first revelations.

The body was photographed in its original position, then eventually removed from the car and placed face up on a stretcher. Anyone who had seen the carnage unleashed on the two previous victims would probably believe the cruelty couldn't get any worse. Well, one look at this decedent would alter their opinion instantly.

Julius glanced at Payne. "See there? These shoeprints are different sizes and patterns. At least three people were here. Most likely one of those shoeprints belongs to the unlucky bloke on the stretcher. We'll know more when we have a chance to study them closer and make a comparison with our shoeprint imaging database."

"Is that his tooth on the ground?" Toombs asked.

"You better believe it, and three more to go along with that. Markers five, six and seven are all teeth knocked from his mouth," Julius said.

"Detective Payne, we have to move quickly with this one. In another twenty minutes or so everything will be pitch black out here," Espinosa said.

"So, what you got for me?"

"I would say he was killed sometime last night. This one is really bad. This man's arms, legs and several ribs are broken, and as you can see, serious trauma to the head and face. He had zero chance of surviving this assault. With that level of injury to his head and legs, he couldn't have made it to the car. He was dead before he got in. Someone had to put him there."

"His intensity grows by the minute. The son of a bitch is loving the cruelty more and more with each kill. It's like he gets off on it," Payne said.

Payne shook her head and took two steps toward Julius. "It appears the beating took place right here. Hopefully, this scene is rich with the killer's DNA. Some type of biological must be left behind. Unless they're professional killers, some tiny part of them must remain here in this spot."

"If anything is here, biological or otherwise, we'll find it, but it's not going to be tonight. We're about to hook up the car now, but we have to come back at first light and go over the scene with a fine-tooth comb. Even with lighting, we wouldn't be able to see a bloody thing tonight," Julius said.

"He has no phone or ID on him. The car is registered to one Alberto Sanchez from Midland Avenue. This is what Sanchez looks like on his driver's license. Pity the stiff's face is too pretty to make a credible comparison," Toombs said.

"Do we know him?" Payne said.

"Oh, partner, you're gonna love this. Sanchez has multiple priors. He bonded out of county three days ago. This one doesn't have Goudy's name on it, but it was Pope's Bail Bond who got him out. Same bail bond as Davidson and Johnson."

"What the fuck is going on in this town? Someone is cutting down these jailbirds, and it doesn't look good. We've got to stop this hemorrhaging, and we have to stop it quickly."

T hough the victim's face was too fractured to assist with his identification, his fingerprints confirmed he was indeed Alberto Sanchez. Patrols were set in motion to cover the area overnight until Julius returned to complete his processing of the scene at dawn.

Toombs had his hands full, taking care of paperwork back at the office before heading home for the night. Payne, on the other hand, took off immediately after wrapping up things in the woods. Her mood was somber while she cruised home. Melodies from Miles Davis's "Blue in Green" simmered softly as she drove. By then the ruby red sky had gone completely dark. It seemed abandoned by both moon and stars.

Payne reflected on the presence of two sets of shoeprints at the scene believed to be the killers. The murder scene showed signs the conflicts between the killers may have been resolved. A cruel sense of synergy existed in the ruthless execution of their latest kill. Whatever disconnect had previously dogged the perilous partners in crime now seem to be a thing of the past. If Payne's speculations proved correct, that deadly duo spelled nothing but horror ahead for homicide.

Daniel sat on the front porch with the lights low and a smoldering cigar between his fingers. Alyssa parked the Ram beside his truck and took her sweet time getting out. Time had no meaning or relevance to her. The cruelty demonstrated by the killers weighed heavily on her mind.

Daniel pulled hard on the cigar then set it aside. He knew firsthand the tremendous burden of her job. having done it for almost three decades. One look and he could tell she was laboring under the pressuring weight of the case. Homicides like the ones currently plaguing the city could be tricky for any detective. Murders where the perpetrators moved so far beyond the pale into the darkened realm of their twisted reality. How in God's name does one remain sane when confronted constantly with men who kill without conscience or morality? Men who derived pleasure from the persecution and murder of their neighbors.

"I can tell today was one of those days," Daniel said.

"I've seen better. How about you?" Alyssa asked.

"What can I say? Turns out retirement isn't so bad after all. Saw the news about the body in the woods. Who stumbled on the corpse all the way out there?"

"Anonymous caller. The assumption is that someone was looking for privacy to get their groove on."

"That's quite a drive for a little necking, don't you think? By the way, I went for a drive today. Wanna know what the streets are saying?"

"Go ahead, Dad. Lay it on me."

"They think the killer is a lot more effective than the law ridding the streets of violent criminals. Taking out the trash, they say. Some even go as far as equating the killer's actions to doing the Lord's work."

"They might say that now, until he grabs one of their own. Bet they'll be singing a different tune then."

"I know this case carries nothing but challenges and tragedy. I also know you're the best detective for the job. Sometimes, you gotta step away for a moment, clear the cobwebs from your head, and start afresh. The answers will come. Just cut yourself some slack."

"I won't argue with that. I'm going up. Goodnight, Dad."

The morning was as bright as Payne was in her khaki pants and brown boots. The air was fresh and sweet like a rose garden when she pulled up at the office. Before she made it to the building, an eerie aura took hold of her. It was the feeling of being followed. Light footsteps tipped closer and closer behind her.

With a quick adjustment to her stance, she whipped her body around to face her follower. There she was, reaching out to touch Alyssa's hand. Alyssa immediate-

ly recognized the approaching woman. Fabian Davidson's mother. Alyssa remembered her from her visit to
Davidson's house. The old woman looked a lot paler
than before with pain and displeasure in her eyes.

"Detective, did you catch the man who murdered my
boy?" the woman asked.

"Not yet but we're working on it. Whenever we get
him, you'll be the first to know," Payne assured her.

"The man who murdered Fabian... I hear them say
he's a hero. Detective, he'll always be a killer in my
book. Fabian was no angel but no one had the right to
kill him. No one."

"You're spot on about that. Whoever murdered your
son is an evil bastard. That's what he is, and I promise
he won't get away with it. I'm going to hunt him down
like any other killer in this town and bring him to justice. Take care now. I'll be in touch."

Payne watched the woman walked away before con-
tinuing into the homicide building. The team was already firing ahead when she got there. Toombs had
his head down digging into the background of Pope's
Bail Bond employees. Payne bypassed her office and
proceeded onto Lieutenant Lorrigan's farther down the
corridor. He was busy on the phone but pointed her
to the chair before his desk while he wrapped up his

conversation. Moments later, he slammed the phone down, lifted his head, and stared her in the eyes.

"Payne, what the fuck is going on under your nose? Aren't you going to catch this fucker before he kills all the jailbirds off the streets?"

"We're working on that. Following a few leads. Hopefully, something will pan out soon. Give us a little time, we'll get him."

"Alyssa, you know that time is never our friend. So far, he dropped three bodies on our doorstep and what do we have to show for it? Not a God damn thing."

"We're working the evidence to the bone. LT, you know we can't rush to judgment in this business. It's going to get hot under your feet for a minute, but we'll nail his ass to the wall in the end."

P ayne dropped into the chair behind her desk. She looked over several entries in her notebook before joining the rest of the team on the floor. Hanson reported on their visit to the Milky Way Ice Cream Shop. Greenwood played the video footage they acquired from the shop. The footage captured Davidson entering, dressed in the same red shirt he had on when his body was found. He bought ice cream and paid in cash. It showed him eating as he exited. He lingered a while on the piazza, snacking on his treat. Davidson shifted his head to his left then stepped out of frame in that direction.

Four customers went in and out during the time Davidson was in view. The last person to exit was a young woman. She left a minute after Davidson went off camera. The woman went outside and turned left in the same direction as Davidson. That was the only visual of Davidson from that night. The shop's small staff were interviewed, but nothing significant was discovered. They recalled Davidson entering and buying ice cream before leaving. There was nothing untoward about the interaction, and nothing suspicious was observed, they claimed.

Payne watched the recording a second time, zeroing in on the last female customer. She used a card to pay for her purchase then exited and walked away in the same direction as Davidson. Payne pondered whether the woman was the witness who called and reported the incident. Payne understood full well if she was indeed the one, her life would be in imminent danger. As far as they knew, this witness may be the only person to get a glimpse of the killer in action and walk away with both kneecaps intact.

"She paid the cashier with her card. Somebody needs to hall-ass over there and track her down before those killers get their hands on her. If they do, it's lights out for her," Payne said.

"As soon as we wrap up here, Hanson and I will head back over there," Greenwood said.

"The tech guys got something off Davidson's phone. They were able to lift a partial print that wasn't Davidson's. They did a run-of-the-mill, but the print didn't match anyone in our database. I'm going through his calls and messages, but so far, nothing stands out," Cruikshank said.

"Perhaps we should expand the search outside the crime database. Go wider. Okay. Let's get on with it then. Toombs, you and me will go check out Sanchez's home in five," Payne said.

"Make it ten. I Need to wrap up this report before we go."

"McBride, now, my office," Payne said, walking off ahead of him.

McBride nodded and gazed across at Cruikshank whose face projected zero emotion. Payne made quick strides down the passageway, and McBride followed. He thought her tone sounded serious and wondered what the hell he did wrong this time?

It felt like being summoned to the principal's office for a detention stint. When he walked in, Payne grabbed his baseball cards from a drawer and handed them to him. After eyeballing his precious collection again, McBride's jaw dropped like a hot Mike. A picture he thought might only be possible in his rarest of dreams. His money was gone for good, but the real value of his collection far exceeded the stolen cash. The sense of restoration to his achievement and pride could only bode well for his shattered esteem.

"How? Where did you get these? This is incredible," McBride said, smiling broadly.

"That story is too long to tell, but I will say this. Fay is gone and so is the cash. This should count for something though. You can put that wretched chapter behind you now. She won't bother you anymore," Payne said.

"I don't have words to thank you. How many times are you going to save my ass from disaster?" McBride said.

"Nobody is counting here, brother."

"You can't always be there, you know. Some of us are just too damaged to recuperate. Too far gone to come back home."

"Don't you give me that end of days dystopian crap. Sometimes things are screwed up, but that's life. It's never too late for anyone to make it back home. Never. So, you promised to go for a sit-down with our shrink. How did that go?"

"It went well. We have another meeting scheduled for next Friday."

"Great job. Keep it up, and let me know if you need anything."

The drive to Sanchez's place was a straight shot on 40. It was a long enough ride but a straight shot nonetheless. Toombs took the wheel while Payne studied crime scene photos on her phone. The myriads of moving parts that were in some way connected to these murders would make anyone's head spin. Most were challenging to follow and seemed destined for a dead end. Sometimes that was simply the nature of the game when it came down to complex investigations. Many a fly-by-night detective appeared on the scene believing fancy suits and a big iron would make the man. The wise ones quickly learned it actually works the other way around. It takes a man or woman with brains and backbone to wear the suits and swing the heavy iron effectively.

Before they drove past the junction with Glenwood Avenue, Payne instructed Toombs to turn.

No doubts existed as to their destination. Fay's Flower Shop was only a short distance in. When they arrived, the colorful signboard was taken down and the front door left wide open. As they approached the door, the smell of fresh paint hit them like a sledgehammer. The inside was all cleaned out.

A cranky-looking fellow stood on a ladder painting the ceiling. He told them the previous occupant gave up the place and left. The shop was being prepared for new tenants. Following that encounter, Payne smiled dryly, realizing that Fay had taken her warning seriously and got the hell out of Dodge. Within the next few minutes, they were back on 40 burning rubber on the road to Midland Avenue.

Midland Avenue was awfully quiet. The street was empty of foot traffic. Besides a lone minivan that passed by, the entire neighborhood seemed fast asleep. As they walked the long walkway to the house, Payne pondered why not even a single neighbor was seen outdoors.

Before she had the chance to think of an answer, a barrage of gunfire erupted from Sanchez's house. Payne and Toombs scrambled for cover and returned gunfire. Within a few seconds of their arrival, the smell of gun smoke consumed the air.

CHAPTER TEN

The blast from a shotgun ripped through the middle of the front door from inside out. Toombs fingered his radio and called for backup. A bald man cracked the door and crawled out on his knees, clutching a shotgun. The front step was as far as he made it after unwisely pointing his gun in Payne's direction.

Payne plugged him with two slugs to his head and shoulder. A second man fled around the back, but he was stopped in his tracks by Toombs in a tactical stance. Toombs ordered him to drop his pistol, but he failed to comply. He decided to roll the dice on his life instead.

Needless to say, things didn't end well for him. Toombs fired twice, and the man slumped forward as the pistol slowly slipped through his fading fingers. Like his friend around the front, he lay dead on the ground with his gun before him.

When all the dust and gun smoke settled, both Payne and Toombs were unhurt. Backup came quickly to find the two gunmen dead on arrival. The premises was searched and another firearm recovered. Heroin and a quantity of counterfeit $100 notes were also seized.

Unpredictability is the nature of the game in police work. One never knows what awaits on the other side of the door. They went to Midland Avenue looking for answers, but today only guns were willing to talk. From what they were able to piece together, Sanchez's cronies probably thought they were being raided by the police. It appeared their best instinct was to shoot their way out. That turned out to be the last bad decision they would ever make. They only managed to shoot themselves six feet into the ground.

It was almost 5 p.m. when Payne and Toombs left Midland Avenue. The tightness in their throats explained the feeling of being shot at unexpectedly. The dead men were identified as Lugo Torres and Frank Perry, known criminal associates of Sanchez. Toombs questioned in his mind, why in hell they were investigating the murders of three known career criminals to begin with? An investigation that nearly claimed his life and that of his partner. Toombs already had the answer to his question, but in that moment, he thought he'd earned the right to query it anyway.

"You alright, partner?" Toombs asked.

"We almost got our asses shot off and you're asking if I'm alright? Fuck no. Ask me again after a gin and tonic. I'll be alright then," Payne replied.

"At least the sun will come up for us tomorrow. There's no more sunrise in the forecast for those two wannabe cop killers."

"What if Sanchez's killers believe they are helping to clean up the city by murdering criminals? Think about it. What if we have a hateful vigilante on our hands?"

"I have an issue with that suggestion. The severity of the injuries inflicted on the decedents tells me it's deeply personal. The killers literally beat the victims to death, breaking bones like twigs. This is definitely something more. Something visceral."

"There's nothing that say both things can't be true about the killer at the same time. They don't have to be mutually exclusive. A vigilante can also have deeply personal motivations for murder. That would explain his unhindered indulgence in the cruelty he rained on his victims."

"Why here? Why now? Why does he hate these men so much? Alyssa, how does he pick them?"

"That we don't know yet. I think we can remove race from the equation. So far, he has killed black, white and Latino. The common denominator with all the victims is that they're all career criminals. All three were bonded out through the same Bail bonds company. Two were bonded by the same pastor. That's what we know for sure. Maybe the men he murdered reminded him of men who wronged him in the past."

"Judging from what happened to us earlier today, I say we can't rule out gang involvement. I'm not saying there is. I'm simply saying we shouldn't rule it out."

"Duly noted. Now, let's get our tails back to the office."

D aniel perched on the porch like a worried father, waiting for Alyssa to roll up the long roadway to the ranch. A glass with bourbon sat on the table yet he hadn't taken a single sip. Sweet melodies from John Coltrane's "My Favorite Things" bellowed in the background but Daniel was numbed to it. He was numb to the world around him.

He still had friends in the police department, so learning of Alyssa's gunfight didn't take long. Daniel knew full well she could handle herself masterfully against formidable adversaries, but she was all he had left, which meant everything to him. It wasn't until he saw the headlights from the Ram snaking up the driveway that he finally allowed the bourbon to burn his tongue.

The night drifted away quietly, giving way to another promising day in Columbus. Daniel seemed in high spirits serving up Alyssa's favorite breakfast. He kept the conversation light and casual, circumventing the heavy worry of the previous day.

The reception at the homicide office was equally special for Payne and Toombs. The rest of the crew wanted details of the shooting. Most importantly, they were expressively happy that Toombs and Payne weren't the ones who got their bellies full of bullets.

Lorrigan stomped in to calm the temperature and settle them down. He couldn't wait until Payne made it to his office to show his support and satisfy himself that they were doing well. Payne made the point that the two cowards who took a crack at them were justly neutralized. And it was time once again to rock and roll with the investigation of the three unsolved murders on their plate.

As part of the administrative process, officers are required to undergo a review following all police-involved shootings. Payne and Toombs had theirs coming up in two hours. They knew it was a good shoot. Notwithstanding, that procedure was instituted as a form of checks and balances and had to be adhered to even if it appeared unwarranted. There was quite a bit stirring with the case. Which means nobody was thrilled about the top detectives being jammed up in a review for hours.

Hanson and Greenwood's return to the ice cream shop earned them a solid with the woman they believed to be the witness. Her credit card information said her name was Mia Chisholm, a resident of Columbus. That lit a spark in Payne's eyes that burned brighter than Venus. All that good news drew one of those rare Alyssa smiles not many had ever seen. They had Mia's address, and Payne needed her found fast. She turned Hanson and Greenwood loose to finish the job and track down Chisolm before less friendly hands got hold of her.

Toombs was the first to face the review panel, which lasted no more than thirty minutes. Once he got going, it was all smooth sailing to the end. This wasn't his first rodeo sitting through a review, and his method remained consistent all the way. Keep the story short and sweet. Telling the truth is always key. Most importantly, layout the facts in sequence of occurrence.

Once the meeting was over; Toombs wasted no time putting distance between himself and that office. Alyssa was making her way in while he was exiting. Toombs flashed her a quick fist bump and nodded as they crossed paths. He hollered to her that he would await her back at the homicide office then continued to his car.

This review exercise wasn't Payne's first sit-down either. It was her fourth shoot, which also meant her fourth review. This one, however, was a breeze for her. She was in and out in well under twenty minutes. The review panel had only a few routine questions, and Payne responded accordingly.

Only one major concern occupied her mind at the moment and wouldn't let it rest. It was finding the witness. She thought of calling Hanson for an update then pondered the distance the detectives had to travel to Mia's home. Patience was certainly not one of the hereditary qualities bestowed on her at birth. It was something she had to cultivate and probably one of the few traits she was yet to excel at. It was definitely an arduous work in progress purposefully propelled to the backburner of her priorities. So, she climbed into the truck and pushed off toward the office. Then her phone lit up with an incoming call from Hanson.

"Tell me you have her," Payne said.

"Wish I could. So, we found Mia's place, but nobody's home. I'm afraid she's in the wind," Hanson said.

"What about her neighbors? What are they saying?"

"She was last seen leaving about nine this morning. They described her as a private person. Quiet, but pleasant and engaging."

"Okay. Stay on it until she returns. Don't you come back here without her."

"We'll be here."

Payne punched a call to Doctor Sherman at the medical examiner's office. She felt she'd seen enough pussyfooting around the case. It was time to get those brutal killers off the street and be done with it.

Sherman indicated a willingness to accommodate Sanchez's autopsy at three o'clock in the afternoon, and Payne happily accepted.

She wished there were more hours in her day. She wished she could be in more than one place at the same time. If any of those things were even remotely possible, she could accomplish so much more in less time. Then reality settled in once again, and with it the understanding that she had to work with the same gravitational boundaries as everybody else. That was a clear acknowledgment that life wouldn't be throwing her any mystical miracles today, or any other day for that matter.

C ruikshank was all flushed in the face when Payne returned to homicide. His long-awaited mapping of the most likely route traveled by the killers was finally completed. All street cameras relevant to that locale were thoroughly scoured in real time. It took significant time and commitment out of him, but he got it done. Hopefully, he'd uncovered something valuable, because Payne was hound dog hungry for a breakthrough. It was time they had a leg up on the most violent killers Columbus had ever encountered. The moment she entered, Cruikshank was ready to deliver what he had.

"So, this is what we gather about the likely route the killers used. From the area near Rhodes Park where Davidson was assaulted to Grove Street where he was dumped is approximately twelve miles. I believe they stayed on the 71 to avoid town traffic cams. I have to admit, this guy is pretty slick."

"In other words, you have nothing," Payne said.

"Are you forgetting how good I am at what I do? He may be good, but I'm a lot better. He was home free on 71, but once he got on Broad Street, his ass is all mine. Look at this gray cargo van here. It goes toward the dump site, and ten minutes later, it turned tail back where it came. The license plate is bogus. Stolen from a Volvo two weeks ago. This isn't a lot, but it gives us something specific to look for."

"Are you kidding? That's a big fucking deal. If the witness put the van near Davidson's attack, we know we're in business. Great job, Detective. This may be the break we've been waiting for."

"I'll bet my paycheck that if we find that van, we find an oil leak under it. You're the man, brother," Toombs said, hitting Cruikshank with a strong fist bump.

Payne immediately made the call to Hanson, giving her the description of the gray cargo van.

From Hanson's end, all movements remained dormant. Mia hadn't returned home since they got there. More and more a sense of concern for Mia's safety started to take hold of the detectives. A BOLO was sent out for the van with stolen license plates. The notification required the seizure of the vehicle and detention of the driver, who was believed to be armed and dangerous. If seen, officers were advised to exercise extreme caution when approaching the vehicle.

Amid it all, Payne remembered her three o'clock appointment for the Sanchez autopsy. She thought of how life always finds it convenient to conjure up inopportune times to throw its curve ball. Life is never constantly smooth one way or the other. One minute things were progressing at a normal pace and the next, all hell broke loose. That may not be all bad, but it certainly makes life a lot more interesting.

CHAPTER ELEVEN

Doctor Sherman conducted an autopsy on Sanchez. His findings were consistent with those of Davidson and Johnson, primarily with regard to their injuries. In this case, the killer's rage intensification was stark. A dislocated jaw and knocked-out teeth made Sanchez's wounds more devastating and extreme than anything they had seen thus far.

The only exception was that Sanchez had defensive wounds to his arms. In all three killings, the victims were physically able to defend themselves, yet the first two bodies had no defensive wounds. Payne believed they were probably surprised by someone they knew. Someone they didn't consider a threat and therefore didn't see coming in for the kill. Sanchez must have seen the attack coming, but apparently not soon enough to alter the deadly outcome that awaited him.

Another thing found on Sanchez that was consistent with the previous murders were the watermarks on his upper body. That still puzzled Payne as to its purpose. What was the meaning of it? Finding the answer to that question would definitely open up a window into the unhinged mind of the murderer. It would speak volumes in terms of his motives for the murders.

Doctor Sherman also removed what appeared to be skin cells from under Sanchez's fingernails. Payne made certain that was whisked away to the lab for analysis. The fact that Sanchez fought his attackers may have contributed to him being beaten more mercilessly than the previous two victims. The anticipation was that some modicum of good would come of it. That he did get his killer's DNA under his nails and possibly other trace evidence on his clothes that the lab would discover.

Payne left the autopsy with plenty on her plate to think about. Three murders in under three weeks would leave a terrible taste in anyone's mouth. Notwithstanding that, the killer seemed to be targeting men with undignified backgrounds. What mattered was putting the pieces together and removing the deadly menace responsible from the city streets.

"The world is getting a lot smaller around this evil bastard. He doesn't know it yet, but the walls are closing in on him," Payne said.

"We'll get him. Pretty soon he'll run out of road, and we'll be right there to scoop him up," Toombs said.

"This thing about watermarks on the bodies keeps bugging me. Why throw water on the men after murdering them? Is it part of his sick ritual? Who the fuck are we dealing with here? Don't tell me it's another crazy wacko."

"What I want to understand is why he targets frequent flyers? What's the likelihood he was a jailbird too? Maybe he's trying to kill the very thing he once was. You know, that part of him he now hates,"

"That's deep. I feel your behavioral analysis side rising to the surface. I will drop you back at the office and swing by to talk to Hanson and Cruikshank at the witness' apartment. Will you look into that partial print from Davidson's phone? See if it fingers anyone."

"Sure thing."

Hanson and her partner sat on Mia's apartment for half the day with negative results. The day continued to drift away but Mia was a total no show. Payne arrived and relieved them from watch. Needless to say, they were more than happy for a change of scenery.

The detectives were left with no other place to look for Mia. Her background check came up empty. Their earlier suspicion of Mia being a stranger to the city appeared spot on. She came to Ohio from Michigan in late December. So far, they'd found no record of relatives, friends, or associates anywhere in Columbus. Mia was currently job hunting; therefore, her apartment was the only known link to finding her. So, Alyssa sat quietly, waited, and watched.

Seven o'clock in the evening drew shadows over the city. Payne hummed softly while adjusting her playlist to the melodies from John Mayhall's "The Mist of Time." Suddenly, her eyes caught sight of a gray cargo van cruising by. The Chevrolet Express slowly drove to the end of the street, turned around, and came back past Mia's apartment. Its wind-up tinted windows restricted the view of the driver and possible occupants. Payne pressed herself back in the seat with her eyes glued to the van. The tag light was out, so getting a good read on the plate from her vantage point drew a blank. She fingered her phone and alerted Toombs. She requested cover and preparation for an intercept.

The Chevy lingered a little before exiting the street. Payne followed from a distance until personnel were in position to execute the intercept. Then she gave the green light.

The stop was surgical. Two marked cars blocked the Chevy's forward path while Payne locked it in from behind. Toombs came up and parked a little behind Payne's truck. Officers held strategic positions with their weapons at the ready. Instructions to the driver were loud, firm, and unambiguous. For a tense moment, the occupant of the van hesitated to comply with instructions to wind the window down. Adrenalin pumped through them, hoping they had their man. Then the driver slowly rolled her window down and raised her hands head high.

It turned out the driver was on the job delivering packages in the area. She was interviewed and subsequently cleared of suspicion in the ongoing investigation. The license plate checked out as did all relevant documentation. The vehicle was squeaky clean. It also came up negative for any indication of an oil leak. At first sight, it checked all the right boxes for the killer's hearse, but in the end, that wasn't the case. Given the circumstances at play, there was no doubt it was the appropriate move to intercept. They drew a dud for sure, which only made them hungrier and more determined to dig deeper in their pursuit for evidence.

It was almost eleven o'clock when all the verification was done to Payne's satisfaction and the driver and van cut loose. Payne shuffled into her overcoat, dropped her partner a solid stare then walked away. Instead of traveling the shortest route to the ranch, she circled back to Mia's apartment on her way there. This time, something was noticeably different. A car that wasn't at the apartment earlier in the evening was parked out front. The curtains were still drawn, but lights were on inside the apartment. The sight of this development instantly struck a chord with Payne, making her eyebrows lift.

She slipped from the truck and started up the palm-shaded walkway to the apartment. She mounted the stairs to the second floor. 27B was in the middle of the building, which climbed its way to four floors.

Payne knocked on the door and waited. No response came. She knocked harder the second time but the result was more silence. Payne pushed the door gently and it swung open. She called Mia's name and identified herself as Columbus Police. She drew her weapon and announced her presence again while she inched her way through the apartment.

Overturned flowerpots on the ground and scattered utensils on the kitchen floor indicated clear signs of a struggle. Most importantly, there was no sign of Mia

anywhere. No sign of anyone inside. This was indeed
another sign that Columbus was a dangerous place. The
only known witness seemed to have disappeared without a trace.

A t first light, Alyssa descended the stairs ready
for work. Daniel's outstretched hand held a fresh
mug of joe from the pot. She scooped the mug and
swallowed a couple of sips. She drew a chair and seated
herself at the table across from Daniel.

A small television mounted on the kitchen wall
played video footage from the scene where the Chevy
was intercepted the night before. The weird-looking
newscaster stated that according to reliable sources
close to the case, the incident was part of a larger investigation into the string of murders committed in the
area recently. It was an understatement to say Alyssa
grew red in the face with rage after viewing the news
report.

"Reliable sources, my ass. This stupid amateur just
blew our case straight to hell. The van is a major lead
that the public need not know about, and now, because
of her, the killer knows we're on to him," Alyssa said.

"Think you have a leak in your house?" Daniel asked.

"I hope not. Got to go, Dad. How the hell am I going to mop up this shit?"

"I know. Someone needs to have words with that reporter though. She needs to know a thing or two about boundaries and responsible reporting."

"I'm afraid if I talk with her, I might be tempted to let my Glock do the talking."

P ayne was less than a mile away from the office when she took a call from Pastor Goudy. He requested she stop by the church for a quick face-to-face. She thought he sounded a tad anxious and rattled. Not the confident and purposefully controlled village leader she'd previously encountered at the church.

Payne considered herself a fairly reasonable reader of people's personality. In Goudy's case, from the first time she heard him talk, she'd found him a less-than-likable human. Much of her perception came about because of the pastor's shifty reticence when confronted with questions regarding the murder victims. He avoided admitting to knowing them, or that any of them were ever a part of his congregants. In her mind, summing up the pastor probably only needed one word—untrustworthy. This softening in his tone gave her cause to ponder his reason for making the call?

Payne spun the truck around, destined for Goudy's church. A few minutes later, she drew down in front of the building. She gazed around for a moment, gathering her thoughts and preparing the mental readiness the crafty pastor demanded. By the time she exited the truck, Goudy had already come out through the front door and marched toward her with his seemingly measured posture. His unbuttoned brown suit jacket swung compliantly with every swaggering step he took.

"Detective Payne, thanks for dropping by so swiftly. It was most audacious of me to impose such a request on you. You know, considering how busy you must be," Goudy said.

"I'm busy for sure, but we still must make time for our citizens. You sounded a little urgent on the phone, though. So, what can I do for you?" Payne said.

"As promised, I asked around about the two murdered men. Young men violently swept away before their time. From what I gathered from my flock, they had a multitude of enemies. Some hungry to exact their personal brand of retribution."

"Care to elaborate? Would do us a world of good if we know what rock to look under."

"I may have heard something about Johnson. That he lifted drugs that didn't belong to him from that shady bike shop on Town Street. Heard the owner swore death on him. They're a nasty bunch, that crew. For whatever it's worth, you might want to lift the lid on that bucket and look to see what's inside."

"Thanks for the word. We'll look into it."

"Detective, I saw you this morning on TV hard at work. They said the driver and seized truck were connected to the murders. That's great detective work on display there."

"That's why I don't watch the news very often. They get too many things wrong. That vehicle had absolutely nothing to do with the murders. Though I can't give details of ongoing investigations, I can say that last night's work was totally unrelated to the case you mentioned."

"How can I be of service? Is there anything or anyone I need to keep an eye out for? My proximity to people on the ground sometimes allows for unique insight, especially if one knows what questions to ask or what to look for."

"You've been very helpful so far, and we'll definitely check into the bike shop. However, beyond what is already out in the public domain, I'm afraid there's nothing else I can comment on. We're basically grasping at straws in terms of suspects right now. Like you said, it could be drugs or perhaps a gang feud. Sad to say but these men, their lifestyle didn't exactly inspire long life expectancy."

"Thanks again, Detective, for coming. I'll be in touch if anything of substance crosses my ears. I can imagine how difficult it must be to solve murders in this city, especially when witnesses are so challenging to find."

The minute Goudy mentioned witnesses, Payne's eyelids lifted like an attack dog's tail. She knew the pastor was shifty, but she never expected him to push the needle this far.

Payne left the church, focused on what she thought was a slippery game of chicken by the clergyman. A fishing expedition into the strength of the ongoing investigation. What she didn't quite understand was Goudy's need to know. Why was he so interested to poke his nose in this case? Though Payne took an early dive into his background and found nothing incriminating, she still considered him an unlikely but possible candidate for the killings. Now that he was snooping around only brought him back under the scope of her spotlight. That was certainly not the kind of luminous spotlight the pastor needed shining on him.

CHAPTER TWELVE

As the Friday morning sun rose, Payne and her team arrived at the Free Wheelers Bike Shop on Town Street. The special operation unit provided support for the raid while the Narcotics Division took lead. Since Narcotics already had the gang surveilled, it was most appropriate they continued to sit in the driver's seat and make whatever arrests became necessary.

It appeared Goudy's tip had some elements of merit to it, though his motives remained ambiguous. A narcotics surveillance team had snapped pictures of Johnson entering the bike shop the day before he was killed. They also captured him leaving the building approximately fifteen minutes later with a small bag slung over his shoulder. Surveillance pictures showed him smiling as he walked away. Whoever murdered Johnson didn't do it at that location. That much was clearly established, considering that the shop was constantly surveilled.

The leader of the rugged bike gang and primary person of interest was a slender shaggy-haired fellow known as Mike Lee. It was believed that Lee and two others were asleep in the building when the officers moved in. First came the announcement of police with a warrant to search. Then the doors were breached and entry made. One of Lee's two sidekicks reached for a gun under his pillow. Then he gazed up and realized that Toombs was miles ahead of him.

Toombs' Glock was already locked on him with its laser light pointed at his chest. The look on Toombs' face was unmistakable. Toombs spoke only four words, but they quickly convinced the biker to stand down. Toombs told the biker to give him a reason. After hearing those words, the biker slowly pulled his hand away from the gun and raised both hands above his head.

Lee and his other sidekick surrendered without further incident. The search left no stone unturned in the biker's den. Criminal charges were well on the way for all three men, which included multiple firearm violations and drug offenses.

Five bricks of heroin and an assorted stash of pills were seized. Several stolen firearms were also recovered. Though the homicide team didn't make the arrests, Payne secured a crack at Lee before he was taken away. She had questions for him about his involvement with Johnson. Lee enjoyed a reputation as a cold-hearted killer and gun runner. Some of the lessons he learned along the way were when to pick a fight and with whom. He definitely wasn't about to confront law enforcement in a fight he was destined to lose. Therefore, his conduct was relatively cool and compliant.

"Why would I kill a man who owes me money? I don't know about you, Detective, but around here, we consider that bad economics," Lee said.

"How much did he owe? I didn't realize you were in the banking business too," Payne said.

"You're a real gem, aren't you? Good looks and a sense of humor are an uncommon combination for a cop. The sucker had me for fifteen large. That's a lot of scratch to lose in one fuckup. Whoever killed him took my money. I tell you this, Detective, you best find the son of a bitch before I do."

"What about your drugs Johnson made off with? I heard you swore to kill him for it. I take it you followed through on your threat. Is that why you broke almost every bone in his body?"

"No way you're pinning that shit on me. What drugs are you talking about anyway? Johnson never stole a single fix. He made a drop for me and got himself killed before he had a chance to deliver my cash. These days murder doesn't make money; it brings unwanted attention and a lot of heat. A whole lot of heat."

It didn't take long before Payne closed the book on Lee. At least for now anyway. Once she satisfied herself that Lee wasn't behind the killings, she closed the curtain on the interview. Payne used the drive back to the homicide office to bring her partner up to speed on the direction she believed the investigation was heading.

"I got a tip and followed up on it. I never thought for a second that bunch was responsible for the murders. Goudy is trying his best to throw us off track. I don't know what skin he has in the game, but I'm sure he's up to no good," Payne said.

"Wanna light a fire under his ass?" Toombs asked.

"Not until we figure out his role in the whole thing. Until then, we act nice and play dumb."

"He really got under your skin, didn't he? What did he do to piss you off so bad?"

"I don't know. I had a murky feeling about him from the beginning, but the moment he mentioned the word witness, I knew the fucker was bad news. You should have seen the look on his face while he threw smoke and mirrors. He pushed so hard to poke his nose into the case it was unbearable to watch. He even asked about the van we pulled over the other night. Trust me, something is terribly wrong about this guy."

"Right now, I say we focus on the evidence we have and leave the sleazy pulpit jigger to his flock. I'm right there with you on him being nosy, but we can't allow ourselves to get distracted. This case deserves nothing less than our full attention."

"No way in hell some halfwit con man is playing me. So, that's what you think is happening here? That I'm distracted by Goudy? Well, I've never been more focused on any case than I am on this one. I'm going to show you how a good detective walks and chews gum at the same time. I'm working this case the way I know, and I'm not letting that snake oil peddler out of my sight either. The real question is, are you gonna be a part of the solution or just a fat fucking distraction?"

The following days brought them no closer to their missing witness, Mia Chisholm. Payne carefully studied the crime scene photographs from Mia's apartment before returning to look for anything they might have missed. Anything that could explain Mia's sudden disappearance. She stood in silence near the middle of the dining room that opened up into the kitchen.

For a moment, she was completely fixated on the splinters scattered on the floor. The point of impact and directionality of the splinters were of particular interest. It dawned on her that there probably wasn't a struggle in Mia's apartment as previously suspected. Swirling inside Payne's mind was the thought that the entire event was purposefully staged. She theorized that someone had stood in one corner and shattered the items on the floor.

As Payne searched the bedroom drawers, she was drawn to two unused syringes from a package of three. All she could think of was that the syringe may have been the method used to extract the drops of blood that sprinkled and smeared the scene. Could Mia really have executed this elaborate plot to shake the detectives from her tail? Mia was the only one capable of shedding light on what had taken place there in her apartment. However, finding this mystery witness was proving to be a tedious task.

Alyssa exited the apartment and slowly turned around full circle. Her eyes swallowed every inch of the adjacent apartments like she craved it. That's when she saw it. The curtains shifted at a window on apartment B across from where she stood. Someone was watching her from the window through the curtains. The window was on the ground floor which made it difficult to miss. The curtains closed as Alyssa got closer. Payne pressed the doorbell and waited. After two more cycles of pressing and waiting without a response, she tried a different approach. She tried verbal persuasion instead.

"Mia, I'm Detective Alyssa Payne. I know how scared you must be of everyone and everything right now. I promise to do everything in my power to keep you safe. Please, open the door and talk to me. You know, you're gonna have to trust someone at some point. You can't do this alone. I'm sliding my card under the door," Payne said.

Payne slipped her card under the door and backed away. She waited a moment, then leaned in for a closer listen. There was a slight shuffle on the inside, which meant her job there was complete. The only thing left for her to do was wait and hope her pitch was effective enough to make a difference. Her eyes tightened with enthusiasm while she regained a full vertical stance. Slow, steady strides carried Payne away from the apartment toward the truck. She must have been halfway down the passageway when the door cracked open behind her. Payne whipped around and locked eyes with the young, stoned-face woman peering back at her.

The tension in the air was as thick as the curtains that draped the windows. Payne hesitated for a second or two, allowing her composure to steady a little. Finding Mia alive meant a great deal to Payne personally, as it did to solving the murders. It was nothing new for her to have a sense of care for her staff and assets alike including people she knew absolutely nothing about. The look on Mia's face told a compelling tale of terror. The kind that said she had seen the callousness of the monsters who wanted her gone. After five minutes of interviewing her, Payne realized she needed to get Mia downtown to homicide. She believed she'd found the key in Mia that could unlock the case and put the perpetrators away for the rest of their lives.

Payne was in great spirits when she stepped into the homicide office with Mia by her side. However, that sense of joy swiftly vanished when her eyes landed on Pastor Goudy gazing back at her and the witness. Goudy was on his way from Lieutenant Lorrigan's office after paying a visit to the man in charge.

Payne's blood boiled in her veins while she pondered what divine vision brought the slithering snake to her place of work. Payne kept her eyes on him until he was completely out of view. Though she was highly suspicious of the slippery pastor, there was one significant fact she couldn't ignore. Mia displayed no negative reaction to Goudy's presence. It appeared he had absolutely zero impact on her. If his being there had any meaning at all to her, then she did a great job of hiding it.

"This guy doesn't know when to quit, does he? Please, will someone tell me what he's doing here?" Payne asked.

"Apparently, he had an appointment with the LT. I heard he's here extending his hand in partnership against violent crimes in the city," Cruikshank said.

"Well, that's a load of crap. Anyone with eyes should see straight through his shabby masquerade. Hanson, this is Mia Chisolm, the witness we've been searching for. Show her to the interview room and make her comfortable. I need a minute to straighten things out with our lieutenant," Payne said.

Chapter Thirteen

P ayne's feelings toward Goudy were steadfast and unequivocal, though evidence to properly sub-stantiate his involvement in criminal conduct was sketchy, vaguely circumstantial at best. Notwithstand-ing, the kick in her gut said he was swimming in the rot all the way up to his neck. Honestly, it wasn't for the lack of trying, but she couldn't kick the probing feeling that plagued her.

Payne stopped in the open doorway at Lorrigan's office while he laughed aloud into the telephone. He waved her in and quickly brought the telephone con-versation to an end. One glance at Payne's raised eye-brows caused his snickers to disappear hastily. They knew the nuances of each other's personalities well enough to recognize that something serious was about to unravel right there between them.

"Alright, what pile of shit do you have to dump on me now? Even a blind squirrel finds a few nuts once in a while, but not with you. In your case, the news is never good, is it?" Lorrigan said, turning his chair around to look Payne in the eyes.

"Don't forget this is homicide, not a likely place to expect daily inspiration," Payne said.

"I've seen that look too many times before, so I know you're here to bust my balls. Say it ain't so. Well, go ahead. Spit it out. What is it this time?"

"Why are you entertaining that sleazy pastor here at the office? You know he's playing you, right? You understand he's only trying to plant his eyes near the investigation?"

"Last I checked, this is still my office. I thought this was my party. I didn't realize I needed your approval about who I admit."

"LT, you know that's not what's happening here. I'm simply saying that man is bad news from beginning to end. I don't trust a hair on his head. If you're smart like I know you are, you'd feel the same way too."

"Okay, Payne. I hear you. Truth is, I don't trust that crowing rooster one bit either. Alright then, tell me what you have on him?"

"I'm working on it. Nothing solid yet, but I know I'm close. I can feel it."

"Until you have solid evidence that will stick on him good, for God's sake, just lay off the guy. By the way, welcoming him within these walls may also have its merits. There's a saying, one should keep his friends close and his enemies even closer."

Payne was about to inform Lorrigan of her success in finding Mia Chisholm when Toombs stormed up and stopped in the doorway. Payne turned and locked eyes with him. Without a single syllable of spoken word, Payne read him well enough to suspect he didn't bring pleasant news. Her eyes briefly shifted to Lorrigan then back to Toombs.

"How bad is it?" Payne said.

"It's Daniel. He was involved in a shooting. We need to move now. I'll fill you in on what little we have on the way," Toombs said.

Payne skipped the office like hell on wheels. Within a minute of Toombs breaking the news, they were racing through the parking lot to the truck. The second they got in, Toombs dropped boot to pedal. Though Payne seemed relatively composed at the moment, her emotions ran rampant and wild in her mind.

"Talk to me. What do you know so far?" Payne asked.

"All we got was that your dad was involved in a shooting on Humphrey. The call was short in length as it was with details. We don't know if anyone was hurt. Basically, we know absolutely nothing," Toombs said.

"Talk about a bad fucking few days."

"Come on, we both know your dad is a wily coyote. It's gonna take a whole lot more than bullets to slow the old guy down. Alyssa, don't you go overthinking things now. We're less than ten minutes out. We'll sort the whole thing out when we get there."

Regardless of how hard Toombs revved the engine, for Payne, it was the longest ten minutes' drive of her life. Her forward gaze was firmly fixed on the horizon off in the distance. The father-daughter dynamics between Alyssa and Daniel had always been strong, but the persistent perils of the last year had definitely forged it in fire.

Deep inside, she knew Daniel's warming up to the lonely life of retirement took nothing away from the love and fascination he found digging for answers. The reality of which meant dangling more times than not in the den of dangerous men. These days, his unwavering motivation was geared toward doing whatever he could to help Alyssa break her tricky case wide open. Gazing off in thought, Alyssa wondered if today would be the day Daniel poked his nose a bit too deep into the trenches and swallowed a belly full of bullets for his snooping. Tires screeched and cried for dear life as they drew down next to a patrol car that awaited them behind the Porcupine Diner on Humphrey Avenue.

"Mr. Payne is seated in his truck over there. Here's his gun. He was not hurt. We checked around but the thugs are long gone," one of the two officers said.

"Thanks a lot for looking out. What actually happened here?" Toombs asked, taking Daniel's firearm from the officer.

"Apparently, two guys tried to get the jump on him but he acted really well under the circumstances. He cracked two at them but they ran like rats."

"Okay. We'll take it from here."

By then Alyssa was already halfway across the little parking lot toward Daniel. He sat quietly waiting in his truck with the door open and his legs hanging out. He puffed hard on his cigarette, smothered the flame between his fingers, then flicked it aside.

The last thing he wanted was to create distractions for Alyssa, but fate continued to prove its propensity to be uncooperative. Sometimes life seemed to give no favors. The moment you start wishing for a break, life steps in with its size twelves and kicks you in the nuggets. Daniel slapped his eyes on Alyssa, marching toward him, and instantly recognized the weight of anxiety she conveyed. He also saw the beauty and joy it gave her to let it go once she confirmed with her own eyes that he was indeed alive and well.

"Dad, goddamn it. You scared me shitless. Shootout in the middle of the morning? What do you think this is, the OK Corral?"

"I stopped by the diner to see Ralph for a quick chat. You remember my buddy, Ralph, don't you?"

"Ralph? Sure. I remember him."

"Well, I stopped the truck right here where you see it. Before my boot hit the ground, two men moved in on me. It's almost like they were here waiting to get the jump on me. I looked around and saw no one else. Customers prefer to park around the front these days."

"Did they say anything?"

"The scrawny fella just kept laughing. One of those ominous laughs that often precedes a kill, and the look on him said he was good and ready for it."

"What happened next?"

"He hugged a piece of iron pipe about three feet long. Said I should hand over my wallet and cigarette. I reached under my shirt and came up with my 45. You couldn't guess what the sucker did then? He laughed in my face, raised the pipe, and asked what was I going to do with the spin barrel? Well, you can guess what happened after. Damn right I lit his ass up. One in his arm and he dropped the pipe and scampered away with his brainless buddy scurrying behind him."

"Where's the pipe?"

"Right there in front of the truck."

Toombs retrieved the pipe left behind by the attackers and recorded a preliminary statement from Daniel. Though neither of the detectives mentioned out loud the likelihood of the pipe being the weapon used in the murders, they undoubtedly entertained the thought. What kind of detectives would they be anyway if they didn't at least consider it? An open mind without rushing to conclusions is key to opening doors in the world of criminal investigations, and no one knew it better than Alyssa and her partner.

They brought Daniel back to the homicide office to see if he recognized his attackers from a collection of criminal mugshots. The last time he walked that corridor the circumstances were even more dire than the ones before him. On the previous occasion, he'd witnessed his best friend and former partner Detective Nelson tragically take his own life. A tragedy that undoubtedly left painful scars on the psyche of so many.

Not long ago, Alyssa thought the progress of the case, along with everything else around her, was moving a little too slow for her liking. Suddenly, all hell seemed to simultaneously break loose., persuasively pulling her in more directions than she cared to encounter. While she worked out the details to formally take Mia Chisolm into protective custody, the day was already beginning to age. At least that meant she would have all the time in the world to sit with her star witness and carefully ventilate every detail of what she saw the night Davidson was killed.

Well, that was the plan anyway. Alyssa sipped coffee from the cafeteria and munched on a blueberry muffin while filling out the form.

Out on the floor, Daniel feasted his eyes on the faces of criminals. He flipped through countless pages of criminal mugshots, searching for a glimpse at the dangerous duo who'd attempted to do him in. Alyssa gazed at the clock on the wall, which said 1600 hours. The day seemed to be running away from her. Perhaps it had witnessed more anguish than it cared to absorb in one day.

"If you were wishing for a touch of good luck, well you got one. We have Daniel's attacker. He showed up at the hospital with a giant slug in his shoulder," Toombs said.

"Get over there and button things up. Take Daniel with you while their faces are still fresh for him. I'm gonna sit this one out for obvious reasons. Let me know how it goes." Payne said.

D aniel said little to nothing on way to the hospital, though Toombs gave ample opportunity to get a conversation going between them, all to no avail. A few grunts summed up the extent of Daniel's reticent responses. Toombs was well aware of Daniel's legacy and unwavering contribution to the homicide department over the years, including his terrible tumble to the exit in the end.

Notwithstanding his dramatic downfall, at that moment, Toombs knew he sat in the presence of true greatness. Pictures of Daniel still hugged the walls of the office. The best clear-up rate on record was realized during Daniel's tenure as the top sleuth at Homicide. Though Daniel's successes preceded Toombs by decades, his respect and admiration for the former detective lived on.

Once at the hospital, Daniel wasted no time finding his voice again. He was first out the door once the wheels stopped rolling, then steered a clear course toward the ER. The second Daniel slapped eyes on the suspect, his fate was sealed. Daniel immediately recognized him as the one who attacked him with the pipe hours earlier. That suggested he probably wouldn't be needing sunglasses any time soon. Considering where his criminal conduct was conveying him, sunshine was least among the things he was about to forfeit anyway.

The faintest thought of parting ways with one's freedom would scare the daylight out of a great many among us. To some frequent flyers in the county jail, their liberty keeps them tethered to the reality of life. Reality of their recurring responsibilities that refused to give them a break. That must be the thing that scares them most of all. Terrified them enough to forfeit the gift of freedom for seemingly senseless petty crimes that keep them going back inside.

For those few, the reality of liberty appeared more constricting than the tiny jail cell that surrounded them. The fact that frequent flyers enjoy almost permanent residency in county jail teased a troubling phenomenon that might only be understood and accurately explained by those who lived it.

Finally, Payne had an opportunity to sit down with Mia in a formal interview. Hanson took Toombs place next to Payne in the interview room. Mia was candid and clear in her recollection of the awful night Davidson was abducted and subsequently murdered. It was a lengthy and eventful day for everyone all around. Even so, Mia seemed restless and eager to unburden herself and tell all to the detectives, who were wide-eyed and ready to listen.

Maybe a little bit of the pressure on her shoulders might loosen once she got that weight off her chest. At least, that was Mia's thinking at the time anyway. As far as Payne was concerned, her keenness to understand the facts surrounding the murders couldn't have come a second sooner. With all the prevailing variables top of mind, Payne set the highly anticipated interview into motion.

"The vanilla ice cream at the Milky Way Ice Cream Shop always tasted great, but that night, it tasted like a little slice of heaven. I settled into the car and went down on the ice cream like a woman in love. That's when I saw the man in the red shirt eating his ice cream across the street from me. He stood a little distance away from the entrance to Rhodes Park. Then, the gray van crept up and stopped in front of him. I don't know why, but I stopped eating immediately. I couldn't take my eyes off any of it. The man. The van. I was transfixed by the whole thing," Mia said.

"Did anything stand out to you about the van? Was there any damage to it? Any writings, markings, pictures, or logos? Anything at all you can remember," Payne said.

"The lighting there on the street was less than luminous, but I'm certain there was a logo on the side that said Parker's Construction. If there were smaller writings, I probably wouldn't have been able to make it out from all the way across the street."

"You're doing a great job. Okay, what happened next?"

"The driver never got out. The man next to him was outside the second the van stopped. He walked over to the man still slurping on his ice cream. They greeted each other like friends. You know, light pats on the shoulders. Then the man from the van swung an object. Something tall like a bat. The poor guy never had a chance. The man whacked him over the head really hard. He went down instantly. Then he pulled out a long blade and went down over the man on the ground. That's when I called 911. I had no doubt death was closing in on him. All I wanted to do was get as far away from there as I could. So, I started the car and drove like a drunk until I was nowhere near that awful place," Mia said.

"The attacker from the van, what did he look like? What about the driver? Did you get a look at him?" Payne said.

"He was white for sure and kind of old. Maybe fifty or so. The front of his head was bald but he had hair on the sides and back. The driver was more cautious. He never looked outside even once. I think he watched the entire episode through the side mirror. At least, that's how it appeared to me now that I'm looking back over everything," Mia said with an exasperating sigh.

More and more, Payne looked at Mia's impeccable memory like a welcomed goldmine. Though often-times, the personal cost of coming forward has proven itself to harbor horrific hazards. More often than any-one would care to admit, unfortunate witnesses have paid the ultimate price for seeing and saying a lot less than Mia recounted.

Payne understood perfectly well that those brutal butchers would likely be gunning for Mia with all they could muster in their attempt to keep her quiet. Hence, her first priority was Mia's safety. Payne was definitely not about to lose this witness. Not today. Certainly not on her watch.

Chapter Fourteen

The world has always been cruel and cold, though it's frequently portrayed as a perfect paradise. Even good people do bad things. On the other hand, bad people seldom fail to inflict their fury, particularly on the humble and the feeble. No wonder many believe it is mostly those who play by the rules who frequently get shafted. The men and women in blue constantly hold the line. Dedicated detectives such as Alyssa Payne and her team were determined to keep their antennas to the ground and their eyes on the evidence. If not for them, the streets could easily become a massacre of the meek. A malicious place where murderers run amok without any contrition or compulsion to account for the enormity of their crimes.

A composite sketch was created for one of the two suspects in Davidson's murder. Though Mia didn't get a closeup look at the perpetrator, she provided pertinent information about his identity. Cruikshank was already all over the van, but so far, his search had run into a brick wall.

There was no Parker's Construction registered in the state of Ohio. None in neighboring states either. Checks on the ground for smaller informal construction companies also came up empty. No one had heard of Parker's Construction here in Columbus. Though Mia presented as a credible witness, this part of her story wasn't quite finding its mark. No one could say with certainty whether this was an indication of cracks developing in her recollection, but it definitely raised a couple of questions for the curious.

"Listen up. I guess it's fair to say, little by little the pieces are finally coming together in this case. The truth is, a statement like that would normally make me happy. Toombs, do I look happy to you?" Payne asked, with outstretched arms.

"That's certainly not your happy face."

"McBride, what about you? Do I look happy?"

"I'd say you look furious."

"Damn right I'm furious. It's true that things are falling into place, but not fast enough. We know way too much to be crawling so slowly behind these heartless hoodlums. These guys are breaking bones like a fucking wrecking ball, and we're here spinning our wheels," Payne said.

"The pieces aren't coming together because we sit on our rumps and spin our wheels. It's because we asked the right questions and followed every lead. As far as I can tell, no crystal ball solves murders. What else should we do?" Hanson asked.

"Fan out and find those fuckers before they kill again. That's what I want you to do. I want that elusive van before it's gone for good. Lean on your sources. Go over everything you think you already know. A diligent detective should remember there's always more than what sits on the surface. Something is always missing, and I need you to break out those shovels and find it. It's far from perfect but get the sketch out there and see if anyone recognizes this son of a bitch," Payne said.

A deafening silence swallowed the room in its giant jaws while Payne walked away. Whether they loved the tone of her delivery or not, they were all busy as bees double-checking everything like she suggested. Perhaps everyone needs a flame lit under their rump every once in a while to keep the blood pumping and the focus aligned with priorities. A frank reminder that in the end, we're all human.

Those who had been around Alyssa Payne long enough understood well that she wasn't one to sit around twiddling her thumbs when the going got tough. She couldn't stand being a spectator in any aspect of her life. Her preference was always to jump in and play the game. Not simply playing either, Payne relished the act of taking the bull by the horns.

Payne's insistence on kicking the sketch of the suspect out in public was her way of shaking the tree and seeing what dropped. She pondered whether the benefits of going public with the sketch would outweigh its associated downsides. If nothing else, it suggested to everyone there was indeed a witness. The move would certainly shine the spotlight once again on Mia Chisolm. Most importantly, Payne hoped the killers might panic and do something reckless. Trying to force the hands of killers was a dicey move for sure, but Payne was banking on them slipping up. Regardless of how brutal these killers were, realizing the law was closing in on them should definitely accelerate their heart rate.

Toombs reached out to forensics regarding the pipe they recovered in Daniel's attack. The lab found no DNA on the pipe except Mark Henry's, the man in their custody for wielding it at Daniel. No trace evidence was discovered linking the weapon to any of the murdered men. The pipe did not appear to have been cleaned or sterilized recently. The conclusion was that the pipe was not the elusive murder weapon they were hoping to get their hands on.

P ayne gazed out her office door onto the extended floor. Her eyes roamed until they landed on McBride seated at his desk. At first, nothing stood out as being even a little strange, up to the point when he shook his head and loosened his necktie. McBride leaned back in the chair, pulled his pistol from the holster, and pointed it to his head.

Payne looked on in horror at the muzzle literally resting on his temple. She thought a valve must have opened somewhere, sending a super surge of blood to her brain. The pen between her fingers slipped her grasp and hit the desk before landing on the floor next to her. By then, Payne was firmly on her feet, running out onto the floor.

McBride struggled with mental health challenges, which the department's psychologist was treating him for. They recognized with genuine concern the treacherous clouds that persistently hovered over his horizon. However, nothing they'd observed suggested he embraced a predisposition for suicide. Alyssa, along with the rest of the team, acknowledged McBride's fragile emotional state. The beginning of his fragility dated back to the death of his mentor, Detective Nelson. They endeavored to keep an eye on him. Apparently, they may have missed some critical signs in his psychological decline.

"John, what are you doing? What's up with the gunplay?" Payne asked, standing a few feet away from him.

McBride turned to face her while Toombs and the others looked on in petrified silence.

McBride chuckled politely. "It's all good. I'm just tired of going around in circles with these soulless killers, that's all. It never ends, does it? No matter how many of them we put away, they germinate ten times faster. Tell me, where does it end?"

"We can talk about the monsters who haunt the city all night long, but you have to ditch the hardware. Hand me the gun and let's talk about it."

"Please, take it before I do something stupid. I'm not sure about anything anymore, Payne. Everything is spiraling out of control around me, and there's nothing I can do to stop it. This is my rock bottom, isn't it? I knew this day would come when I finally ran out of road."

"Don't worry about any of that stuff. You did the right thing. We're going to get you all the help you need. We'll be right here for you through this. We love you, brother." Payne took his gun and hugged him hard.

The entire team converged in a tearful show of support for their troubled colleague and friend. Payne peered over McBride's shoulder and locked eyes with Lieutenant Lorrigan gazing down on them. Something in his eyes said he was beginning to feel the combined pressure of the unsolved murders and internal misfortune plaguing his precinct. With his top detectives already in play, all Lorrigan could do was pray the unlucky spell was temporary.

Pervasive misfortune could be a career killer for anyone, even for a hard-talking, no-nonsense lieutenant like Lorrigan. He understood the chain of command quite well, from the captain above him all the way to the very top. He also recognized the department was under constant scrutiny from various fronts. Undeniably, his success or failure was inextricably linked to the performance of the men and women on the ground. Lorrigan's acknowledgment of the big picture was a reality nobody needed to remind him of. Perhaps his evenhanded approach to the job helped to mold him into the respected manager he became.

The smooth melodies of Dexter Gordon's "Body and Soul" simmered soft and smooth at the ranch while Daniel and Alyssa sipped cold ones on the porch. This was their first sit down at home since the attempted mugging incident with Daniel. The heat was on for everyone, and Daniel and Alyssa were no exception. Though they had both seen their fair share of action over the years, being violently attacked like Daniel had been was not a normal expectation for a man mellowing into retirement.

"So, I understand the guy who jumped you is singing like a bird now. Gave up his buddy and all. The moment he learned who you were, he suddenly had a change of heart. I wonder why that is?" Payne said.

"Did he say what his motivation was? Wait, let me guess. He was craving bullets, wasn't he?" Daniel asked.

"Really, Dad. You're dropping jokes about it. It's a serious matter. You could have been hurt, or worse."

"Okay. What did he say?"

"He claimed they needed quick cash to score a fix. The guys looked into them. They are far too stupid to come after you personally. They're just junkies looking for a random mark to rob."

"That's some wretched luck, isn't it? Of all the people in Columbus, they picked me. Guess I should feel really special they singled me out?"

"Dad, this case got me wondering what the hell I'm missing. I know we're closing in, but I believe we should be seeing things a lot clearer by now," Alyssa said.

"They say the darkest hour is just before dawn. With all the obstacles blurring your path, I suspect dawn in this case may be sooner than you think."

"You know, I took a big risk releasing the sketch today."

"I'm pretty sure you have good reasons to put it out. It's a lot better than the alternative, anyway. Doing nothing is generally the option for least consideration."

"There are at least two suspects out there. That much we know. I'm banking on the sketch creating some friction between them. Any discomfort or anxiety among them must be considered a win for us."

"I see. You're betting on the no honor among thieves doctrine? That's some ballsy move, rattling the cage of the killers," Daniel said.

***

Later in the night, Alyssa lay in bed with her eyes focused on the ceiling. Agonizing memories of a broken McBride overwhelmed her mind and made it grim. Replaying how the ambulance slowly rolled away with him inside inundated her eyes with tears. That wasn't an activity she indulged in for fun, but yes, she cried. She contemplated what the future had in store for him.

What would become of the young enthusiastic detective? He loved the job completely and had paid a hefty personal price for his commitment. Apparently, McBride was incapable of separating the enormous emotional turbulence of his occupation from his own personal life. He carried the burden of the job with him everywhere. In the end, the load proved far too burdensome for his brain. Little by little. Piece by piece. It disillusioned and decimated him. The hazards of the job rendered no mercy for the unlucky detective.

For Payne, dawn came quickly. In some ways, it appeared she closed her eyes in the night, and the next minute, she was looking at daylight. It's often said that time flies when you're having fun. In this case, time seemed to fly, but nothing about the case was fun for Alyssa Payne.

She was on the road to work a touch earlier than usual. Her night had been a little strange and by first light, she was itching her heels to head out. The horrific nature of the murders played a dreary ballad in her head. Shattered bones and battered ligaments. Bodies brutally bent out of shape with missing fingers and teeth. The phrase overkill was a mammoth understatement to the level of cruelty endured by the decedents. It was easy to suspect that when death finally found them, they'd accepted it with open arms. Anything to end the enormity of their anguish.

It took the ringing of Payne's phone to wrestle away the haunting thoughts that gripped her. A quick glance made her realize the incoming call was from none other than Pastor Goudy.

"How can I help you, Pastor?" Payne asked.

"Hello, Detective Payne. Sorry to trouble you so early in the day but my urge to render my service wouldn't let me rest," Goudy said.

"We're always appreciative of any assistance that comes our way."

"I saw the sketch of the man you're hunting. I shared it in church and implored my congregants to come forward if they learned anything relating to him. Tell me,

Detective, is this man the monster behind the murders?"

"All I can say is that he's a person of interest, and we would very much like to talk with him."

"He must be one of those lone wolves as you detectives like to call them. My reason for prying is that our citizens are restless. They need to know their communities will be safe once again when you eradicate him from our streets."

"Right now, the man in the sketch is our primary focus. The rest, I'm afraid, we'll simply have to wait and see."

"By the way, that little word I left with you, I learned it bore fruit. I heard you arrested the leader of that horrible motorcycle gang along with his cronies."

"Yes, we did. I don't believe I had the opportunity to thank you for the tip. So, thanks. We couldn't connect them to any of the murders, but we got them for other crimes. Whatever you learn about the man in the sketch, feel free to reach out."

"Take care, Detective. God be with you. I'll continue to pray for your safety while you hunt these vicious criminals," Goudy said.

"No thanks on that. I'll do my own praying," Payne said as she hung up.

She dropped the phone on the seat, shook her head, and smiled. Not a single word from the pastor's lips felt genuine. If anything, the call made her ponder what sinister motives moved the slippery man of the cloth to come prying once again?

Instead of driving straight to the office as originally planned, she turned onto Central Avenue then onto Wendell Avenue. She gazed at the lonely house Goudy called home. It sat on a one-acre lot with a beautifully maintained lawn. The property boasted imposing oak trees that overlooked the roadway to the east and north. The recent renovation of the house gave a fresh appeal to its old design. Payne gazed about and saw absolutely no movement on the property. No car outside the garage and no one anywhere, so she moved on.

Payne's next stop was the Guiding Light Tabernacle in Franklinton. Goudy's red Cadillac was parked out front sandwiched by two other vehicles. Like Goudy's home, an empty quietness prevailed. On this occasion, the silence was short-lived when a man dressed in blue overalls drove a motorized lawnmower around the lawn. An unlit cigarette tucked in his mouth drew a small chuckle from the otherwise stoic Payne. One sight of the camera pointing down from the church at the parking lot was enough indication for Payne to drive away.

As much as she didn't trust Goudy, she wasn't ready to confront him without solid evidence. Enticing as it was, those were the types of rookie mistakes she avoided. With nothing but finding evidence on her mind, she pressed pedal away from there to the homicide office.

Payne sat in her office rewatching Mia Chisolm's interview on the computer. Approaching footsteps from the corridor drew her attention toward the doorway. Lieutenant Lorrigan stomped in with a weird look on his face and two sheets of paper in his hand. At least, that was the picture Payne observed when she gazed up at him. His unreadable half-smile instantly had her scratching her head for a moment. Though, on this occasion, curiosity wouldn't keep her waiting long before all the answers flowed in like a broken dam.

"Payne, we caught a break with the sketch," Lorrigan said.

"No kidding. Where did it come from?" Payne said.

"Before I answer that question, don't you want to know who it's pointing at?"

"Damn right, I wanna know. I want to know it all. Hook, line, and sinker."

"The sketch matched up almost perfectly with Otis Pope. Get this. Otis Pope is the owner and operator of Pope's Bail Bonds. Here, see for yourself. It's up to you to do the legwork now. We need to be sure he's as good for it as his picture looks next to the sketch." Lorrigan handed Payne a printout of Pope's driver's license and the sketch.

"You're right. This is big. We'll get right on it. This might be the major turning point we needed. LT, where the devil did this tip come from?" Payne asked, studying the sketch and license.

"The tip came from the man you almost accused out-right of pulling off the murders. That's right, Goudy called about twenty minutes ago."

"Goudy?"

"I was just as surprised when he called. He said some-body slipped a note in the collection plate. I guess we take it where we get it, don't we?" Lorrigan said, leaving Payne in a cloud of silence.

CHAPTER FIFTEEN

Despite having little or no faith in Goudy, Payne knew they had to work the tip as hard as they would any other. Too much was riding on identifying the suspects in this case. That was the only way for Payne to stop the murders that laid siege to the streets of Columbus. By putting the perpetrators behind bars or putting them into the ground. Some would gladly argue in favor of the latter as the most suitable option for killers void of redemption or remorse.

Payne assembled the team with a sense of urgency and broke the news about Ronald Pope's likeness to the sketch. The energy in the office immediately exploded through the roof. Eager ears were cocked. Wide-open eyes followed Payne's every motion. Everyone stood ready to hit the ground running and do what they did best. In an almost poetic spectacle, it appeared the stage was set and the players stood ready to perform their roles.

The first assignment was for Cruikshank to match the partial fingerprint from Davidson's phone to Ronald Pope's print. Payne pointed out that Pope had to be fingerprinted to run his bail bonds office. That meant his prints were already on file waiting to be collected and analyzed. A positive result would literally provide probable cause for the requisite warrants they would need to execute.

Hanson and Greenwood were tasked with the excavation of Pope's entire life. Every documented piece of his existence instantly became the subject of scrutiny. It was open season on every aspect of his life. That was quite an elevation for the local businessman who, until today, never entered the homicide detectives' radar.

Payne and Toombs settled down to the business of sticking covert surveillance on Pope's home and bonds office.

"Hold up a minute. There's something you should know about this great breakthrough we're working. More specifically, who delivered it," Payne said.

"Alyssa, what's going on?" Tooms said.

"It came from Goudy. Don't get me wrong. I'm not saying the tip is bad. I'm saying I don't trust his motives. We have to work everything by the book from start to finish. Could be I'm completely wrong about the guy.

Nevertheless, until I'm satisfied that he's clean, we take no chances with him."

"I understand you don't care much for the guy, but so far, the lead looks solid. As long as the tip is good, I say screw his motives. We might even have this case wrapped up by nightfall if everything shakes out right. I'm going to see if Pope has a van registered that fits our case," Toombs said.

"Good thinking about the van. Get on that straight away, brother. I'll get eyes on him and his properties in the meantime," Payne said.

Morale in the office was sky high as they buckled down to work on nabbing at least one of the city's most brutal murderers on record. Payne made a quick call to Mia Chisolm and informed her of the likelihood of her attending a lineup. Though Mia wasn't the least bit thrilled about being on the other side of a mirror from such vicious men, she stood willing and ready to brave it. Payne considered Mia among the most fearless witnesses she'd ever encountered.

"Bless her heart," Payne whispered, leaning back in her chair for a moment.

Payne closed her eyes briefly and reopened them to find Lieutenant Lorrigan standing over her for the second time of the morning. This time, his expression gave everything away. He was there for answers. The stiffness on his forehead screamed impatience. Seeing Lorrigan so rattled was unprecedented for sure and somewhat awkward to watch.

Internal politics within large agencies was never uncommon, and the CPD was not exempted from that reality. At times, it requires next to nothing to rachet up intensity among ambitious players. For Lorrigan, a great deal was riding on the success of this case.

On this occasion, competitive pressure appeared to be the source of his apparent Achilles heels. He recognized that the enormous successes of the Homicide Department in recent years had made it one of the most coveted spots in the agency. That meant security of tenure was not guaranteed for anyone. Whispers traveling through the grapevine suggested there was blood in the water and sharks were already circling for his job.

"Payne, I just got off the phone with the commander at special operations. He's making a team available whenever you're ready to roll. Keep me updated on your progress on this one. If Pope as much as farts, I want to know what he ate for breakfast," Lorrigan said.

"Sure thing. Right now, we're covering all the necessary bases. I'll let you know as soon as we have something to move on. If Pope is the killer, we'll get him."

"No, no. There's no if about it, Payne. We have to solve this one, and fast."

I t was almost an hour into the rush when Cruik-shank finally accessed Pope's fingerprints. It was a definite match to the partial found on Davidson's phone. With that development, Pope's arrest warrant and warrants to search his home and bonds office were already being written up.

DMV records showed a gray Chevrolet cargo van was in fact registered to Pope's Bail Bonds. At long last, it appeared the floodgates were finally opened. The dominos began to fall on the killers, and it felt fantastic to the detectives. The emergence of the groundswell of evidence played beautiful melodies to Lieutenant Lorrigan's ears. Though the dive into Pope's background didn't uncover much of a criminal history, it did trigger a myriad of questions. Much like Pastor Goudy, Pope's life traced back to 2013 and abruptly dried up.

T he entire office was abuzz with preparation for the highly anticipated raids. Time appeared to trickle on at a snail's pace while they waited for the warrants to be signed. Eventually, the warrants got the signature they needed, and before the ink could dry on them, everything was a go.

The surveillance contingents already in place reported no movement at any of the two targeted locations. The bonds office didn't open its doors for business all day and no one had eyes on Pope at his home or anywhere for that matter. In terms of pinpointing where Pope actually was, his home seemed the most likely of the two locations. Of course, Payne had no problem with any part of that picture. If anything, it appeared a little poetic, apprehending such a ferocious killer in his own dwelling. It was no challenge to envision a sense of justification in stripping away his power at the personal space many considered one's sacred sanctuary.

P ayne and Toombs arrived at Pope's home with a team from special operations while Cruikshank and Hanson converged on the bonds office with the second team.

What unfolded at Pope's home was a real shocker for sure. His 2002 Lincoln Continental was parked in the driveway. Payne laid a hand on the hood. As anticipated, the engine was as cold as an icicle. The announcement of their presence outside the house yielded no response from inside. They attempted to breach the front door by force but quickly realized it was left unlocked.

The special ops team were generally the ones to enter and clear the buildings, but Payne and Toombs were right there with them every step of the way. They entered the house with tactical precision, clearing their way in one room at a time. The minute Payne stepped into the garage, the unmistakable smell of death swallowed everything in its reach. Ronald Pope had been murdered in his garage with rusty scissors stuck in his chest.

Pope slumped slightly backward in an orange-colored wicker armchair. At first glance, the picture appeared purposefully staged to make it appear he was staring up helplessly at his scissors-wielding executioner. Payne remained completely motionless for a moment, scanning and studying the scene, her mood grim. Disappointment filled her. She wanted the killer caught and brought to justice, not butchered in his garage.

"Get comfortable, we're going to be here for a while. We need to go over every inch of this place," Payne said to Toombs.

"Clearly, somebody got to him before we could. From the look of it, somebody with plenty of rage and an urge for murder," Toombs said.

"More like someone who didn't want him talking to us. What do you make of this crime scene? Look at this table in front of him. There's only one beer bottle, and I'm sure it has his print on it. That watermark on this side was left by another bottle, but where is it now? There, see those marks on the floor? That chair was right here. Pope wasn't alone. He was drinking beer with someone, and it was someone he knew."

"I already called crime scene and the medical examiner's office. His killer must have left something behind for us. I'm not going to lie; there's no tears in these eyes for that piece of trash. If you ask me, I would say he had it coming anyway. It was only a matter of time until karma came back to collect."

"Don't even think of dropping the ball on this investigation. This has nothing to do with what you think of the guy. We must dig into this homicide as diligently as we would any other homicide. If we don't solve his murder, we fail everything and everyone who suffered at their hands," Payne said.

The search of Pope's home was slow, deliberate, and thorough. Early in the search, they realized they weren't the first ones to rifle through the premises. Pictures missing from photo albums and pages ripped from Pope's diary gave some indications something was amiss there.

The fact that almost every area of the house was rummaged through left little doubt the place had already been searched before they arrived there. Julius and his crime scene crew took their time processing the scene. Though the dead man's cell phone and laptop were not recovered, there was plenty of evidence for the lab to bag and tag.

Payne found a shoulder patch hidden in the back of a drawer out in the garage. She suspected it belonged to some uniform and had the words ONE LAW stitched into it. The letters RP were embroidered with blue thread below the much larger words. Payne theorized the letters RP could the initials for Ronald Pope. Though no one knew its origin nor its purpose, Payne snapped a picture of it on her cell phone before passing it on to Julius.

It wasn't long until the medical examiner's vehicle rolled into the driveway. Dr. Sherman's estimated time of death was 10 p.m. the night before. That gave Pope's killer plenty of time to ransack the house, remove whatever he wanted, and cleanup after the murder.

Sherman's preliminary assessment found no defensive wounds on the body. That finding further solidified Payne's suspicion that Pope was killed by someone he knew and probably trusted. A surprise attack Pope didn't expect and never saw coming. That type of blatant betrayal spoke volumes about the sinister nature of the man she believed perpetrated the entire string of murders in the city.

The minute Cruikshank and Hanson gained entry to Pope's Bail Bonds, they were convinced they were at the right place. A gray Chevrolet van that matched the one they sought was parked around the back. Evidence of long-term oil leaks were visible on the pavement underneath the van. Once they located the keys hanging on a wall in the office, they opened the doors to the van.

Inside the back, they found seven sets of stolen license plates including the one caught on camera the night Davidson was abducted and murdered. Several huge magnetic business logos that represented various fictitious companies were also recovered. One in particular grabbed their attention—Parker's Construction Company. That was the same logo Mia Chisholm mentioned in her statement to the detectives.

If there was any doubt about Pope's involvement in criminal conduct, it all dissipated the minute they saw the contents of the van. All that evidence pointed to extraordinary planning and, quite possibly, premeditated murders. An organized approach that may have started months or possibly longer prior to the first body being found. The question that puzzled Payne's mind most was the bondsman's motives for targeting his victims. What propelled him and his accomplice to unleash such hate and carnage on the men they murdered?

By the time they finished sifting through everything at both locations, Payne was already seeking warrants for Pope's phone records and office computer. Lieutenant Lorrigan and other like-minded folks celebrated the development as a major success in the case. Some went as far as flirting with the notion that the case should be closed since the main perpetrator was confirmed deceased.

Based on the abundance of evidence that pointed to Pope, Lorrigan seemed to believe the rest might simply be preparing the requisite reports and filing paperwork. Lorrigan expressed real enthusiasm as he galloped away joyfully on his long-awaited victory lap.

Payne, on the other hand, pushed back hard against any compulsion for a premature conclusion to the case. She suspected they were being intentionally played like a fiddle. Manipulated masterfully by the man she believed to be the mastermind of the entire conspiracy for the murders. That man she thought was none other than the shady pastor, Goudy.

CHAPTER SIXTEEN

Watching the sun go down at the ranch was always an exhilarating experience for those fortunate enough to witness it. This Sunday evening's view was no different for Daniel and Alyssa as they sat leisurely on the porch. Glasses of bourbon blended perfectly with the fading scent from Daniel's oversized cigar.

Alyssa showed Daniel the picture of the patch she'd snapped at Pope's garage. For a while, Daniel seemed hopelessly trapped in time. Befuddled by the memories of unpleasant encounters left buried in the boneyard of time. Looking at the patch brought Daniel back to 1995, when he was a rookie beat cop trying to find his place in the CPD.

He recounted several young men and women going missing in the area. Most of the missing were teenagers who frequented malls and arcades. It took investigators years to unravel how the youngsters were targeted, recruited, and indoctrinated in hatred. In the end, the players of the cultlike group responsible were never convicted. That meant they never spent a single day behind bars for their unscrupulous actions.

Detectives working the case located the group's hideout but it was too little too late, especially for the elderly couple who owned the farm the group allegedly commandeered. The farm was owned by Eugene Walsh and his wife, Maud. The property was well off the grid, tucked away two miles deep into the woods, which made it ideal for the dreadful bunch who set up shop there.

When police finally found the farm, the group had already moved on. The partially decomposed remains of the couple were discovered buried in a shallow grave. The buildings were set ablaze and burned to the ground.

The group's mission was to be tougher on criminals than law enforcement could ever be. They believed those committed to a career of crime had forfeited their right to life and must be eradicated. Over time, the missing people simply reintegrated into society with no rational explanation of their whereabouts during their absence.

"Wait a minute. Are you saying someone willfully indoctrinated the missing teens to become murderous vigilantes?" Payne asked.

"That was the conclusion at the time. After the two bodies were dug up, detectives really started to look into the group, but it was much too late. The tribe seemed to have dissolved. The only thing I can say for certain was that nobody had anything to say about what happened on the Walshes' farm. The youngsters stridently denied ever being on the farm or being a part of the group."

"What do you mean 'conclusion at the time?' Are you saying you think differently about the case now?"

"I still believe the whole episode about the indoctrination and all. However, I'm a bit foggy when it comes to the part about the Walshes being innocent ranchers who were killed for the occupation of their home. You see, this entire incident has haunted me over the years. What if the Walshes were the masterminds for the group? Think about it. Something could have happened that caused the flock to turn on the shepherds."

"You think the pupils killed their teachers, buried them, and burned the temple to the ground?"

"It's just a thought, but yes. That would explain why none of them talked. They were all complicit in the murders. Now they're all grown up and roaming around out there."

"The only problem with that assumption is that there's no evidence to substantiate any of it."

"Tell you what. Before you shut it down completely, there's someone you should meet. Promise it won't take long. What do you say? Let's go for a ride."

"Dad, I have a lot going on right now. I'm not at all jacked up about chasing ancient mysteries."

"Well, you asked about the patch, didn't you? The most likely way to discover if there's any connection between Pope and the patch is to follow the ghosts of the past," Daniel said.

"Okay, Dad. Let's take that ride," Alyssa said.

As the beauty of the evening sky gave way to the shadows of the night. Daniel and Alyssa drove for a little under an hour. About a mile before reaching Hamilton Avenue, Daniel turned off West Broad Street onto a dusty, unpaved road.

Alyssa glanced across at her dad with an inquisitive countenance that suggested she had questions. Whatever itched inside her head, she kept it to herself. Alyssa remained silent as shifting gravel grumbled noisily beneath the tires. Daniel pulled up in front of an old rundown junkyard. Floodlights spread out sparsely around the property, surrounded by eight-foot chain-link perimeter fencing. Discarded vehicles were stocked atop each other in what could be described as a dilapidated graveyard of cars.

Lights in the front office gave away movement inside through the windows. A burly fellow walked across the office toward the front door. After a few seconds elapsed, the door opened and a massive man emerged outside. With slow, sluggish steps, he dragged himself to the gate. He looked long and hard at Daniel before he wrestled the gate open. Without uttering a single word, the man turned around and headed back to the office.

Daniel gazed across at Alyssa and signaled for her to follow as he exited the truck and moved toward the office. Once inside, the smell of motor oil and old used vehicle parts took over.

Alyssa's eyes found the man seated behind the desk and stayed on him. The severity of his disfigurement made it virtually impossible to look the other way. He was burned from head to toe. From the look of it, his skin had melted away like butter in a skillet. The man switched his gaze from Daniel to Alyssa. As he moved, his physical deformity made it possible to see his eyes shifting in their sockets as he juggled his gaze from one person to the other. A less-than-flattering laugh escaped his twisted lips as he drew on a cigarette and coughed exhaustively like a man ready to kick the bucket.

"He didn't tell you, did he?" the man said, staring Alyssa down.

"Tell me what?"

"He didn't tell you he was bringing you to see the junkyard scarecrow. That you were fixing to meet the abominable freak from the furnace."

"Why would he tell me that? All I see is a man. A man who has been to hell and back," Alyssa said.

"Aw, you're right about that one, Missy. I've been to hell alright. That's exactly where I've been for the last twenty-seven years," the man said.

"I'm really sorry to hear that."

"Policeman Payne, how many times must I tell you not to come back here? You refuse to believe that I had nothing to do with the murders on the farm. I had nothing to tell you then, and I have nothing to say now," the man said.

"Lattimore, this time I bring you good news. Ronald Pope is dead. There's no reason to keep his secrets anymore. I'm not here about the Walshes today. Far as I'm concerned, they were terrible people anyway. Just tell me what you know about the dead bondsman," Daniel said.

"Policeman Payne, you think I'm scared of anyone? That I'm carrying their water? What can they do to me now that they haven't already done? I know you believe I played a role in the Walshes' murders. Truth is, you really don't know Jack shit about what happened out there on that farm," Lattimore said.

"Mr. Lattimore, I have a question for you, if you don't mind?" Alyssa said.

"Aw, beauty and grace. You want to question the monster, do you?" Lattimore said.

"No. Not at all. I want to question the man who wears those painful scars. The man on the inside of that tortured mask."

"Get on with it then. Ask your questions, and then leave me the hell alone."

"Tell me about you. What happened to you out there? Who gave you those barbeque scars?"

"Just when I was getting to like you, Missy. Who the blazers are you, my shrink? Knowing about me will do no good for anyone. Though, I gotta say, you're the first person to look at this old pot-roast in a long time, let alone ask about my crispy shell."

"I asked because I want to understand what happened to you and who is responsible for all your hurt. Earlier you asked what more could they do to you that they haven't already done? Tell me. Who were you alluding to?"

Lattimore pushed his shoulders back into the soft fabric of the huge chair. Though the cushions were generously soiled with grease and probably oil, they seemed comfortable to the man with first- and second-degree burns over every inch of his body. Lattimore sucked in air and savored it like it was sweet to him. He flamed up another cigarette and stared Daniel dead in the eyes. He turned his gaze to Alyssa and settled on her. Alyssa's gaze locked on him until his trembling lips uttered the first tortured word of his account.

Lattimore's story was as heartbreaking to hear as it was to watch him tell it. The beginning of his worst nightmare dated back to 1995. He was only fifteen years old back then. As some teenagers do, he acted out and rebelled against the entire world and everyone in it. When the opportunity came for him to join like-minded teens at a ranch in the middle of nowhere, he jumped at it without a second thought.

Before he knew it, he was the thirteenth teen in a group out in the woods. They were under the guardianship and mentorship of Eugene and Maud Walsh, self-proclaimed founders of the One Law Freedom Club. The group's grooming and training gradually intensified for the better part of that year until it became too much for the teens to handle.

The Walshes believed in a doctrine of self-governance. One that was strong on those who takes the property of another without rightful authority to it. They preached daily that thieves serve dual purposes, to kill and destroy. Therefore, it was up to the strong to ensure their extermination before they have the opportunity to make good on their true nature. One by one, they must confront their demise. Day in and day out, the teens feasted on that doctrine of death until the Walshes attempted to turn their wrath in their direction.

Lattimore recalled the morning Ronald snagged a bottle from the Walshes' moonshine shed and made light work of it with the other youngsters. That single act of dishonesty didn't take long for the Walshes to figure out, given the smell of liquor on the teen's breath. Lattimore, being the only one who didn't partake in the looted liquor, instantly became the prime suspect as the one who ratted out the others to the Walshes.

The year-long grooming made the teens super vigi-
lant and ready to draw first blood. Within minutes, Lattimore was hogtied along with the Walshes and tossed
aside while the young group deliberated on their fate.
In the end, the Walshes were buried alive in a shallow grave by the young monsters they'd created and
nurtured. The first-time killers decided to go their sep-
arate ways and pledged never to speak of that place
ever again. Their final act of evil as a group was to set
the buildings ablaze. As punishment for their suspected
snitch, they tossed Lattimore into the flaming moonshine shed preceding their hasty exit.

"I smelled my body burning that morning. Smelled
like rotting roadkill roasting on a woodpile. My God, it
was horrible," Lattimore said.

"You called the guy Ronald. Do you mean Ronald
Pope?" Alyssa said.

"We didn't use last names on that farm. The One Law
patch was our bond of brotherhood. Even so, I can say
without an ounce of doubt that Ronald and the bondsman are one and the same."

"So, how did you escape the flames?" Alyssa asked.

"Believe it or not, Pope doubled back and got me out
of there in the nick of time. Well, what was left of me
anyway. The son of a bitch listened to his conscience for

the first time in his miserable life. It would have been better if he'd let the flames finish the job and turn me to ashes. The pain was far worse than a thousand deaths."

"Lattimore, what they did to you out there was awful. Do you remember the names of the other eleven teens who were there? Was one of them Vincent Goudy?"

"Don't you dare speak that name here again. Enough digging into the past for one day. Time to go, Policeman. You too, Missy. Don't bother coming back. I've got nothing more to tell. Go now," Lattimore said.

Nothing but unadulterated horror shone through Lattimore's eyes. No words were required to explain his agony. A sorrowful silence consumed everything as Alyssa and Daniel headed outside. They needed time to process their experience inside the office. Whatever was rumbling through their minds remained unspoken. At least for the moment anyway. It wasn't until they were back on the main road that the verbal interactions between them resumed.

"How long have you known Lattimore?" Alyssa asked.

"Too long. I've been trying for years to get him to talk. Until tonight, he never gave me more than two or three unhelpful words. Somehow, you didn't even need two minutes to bust him wide open. Poor guy never even knew what hit him. You did good," Daniel said.

"You saw his reaction when I mentioned Goudy? The brotherhood patch is the connection between Pope and Goudy, don't you see? Once Lattimore calms down, we have to go back and talk to him again."

"I was right about the Walshes being involved. I simply couldn't prove it. Now you have a shot at shining light on it. The only problem with going back is whether Lattimore will talk to you again," Daniel said.

CHAPTER SEVENTEEN

P ayne soaked in the scenery of the homicide building from the driver's seat of the Dodge. Moments
later, she entered the office like she'd done countless times before. Somehow, that Monday morning felt
completely different from the others. Perhaps it was
more consequential to the goals she needed to accomplish.

One glance at Lorrigan's office reminded her of the
hurdles poised to hinder her progress along the path
she'd opted to pursue. The stakes in the case could never have been higher. Hence, picking her battles carefully might be the key determinant between soaring to
the sky or sinking in the sand. Not only was carrying
the investigation to a satisfactory conclusion becoming
more complex by the minute, but success itself started
to seem like different things to different people.

Payne pulled her team together amidst the tsunami
of evidence that had engulfed them since Ronald Pope's

demise. So many of the missing pieces were finally falling into place. Notwithstanding all the tremendous progress made, two key elements of the investigation remained a mystery. The first was finding the murder weapon. Secondly, establishing a clear motive for the murders was still a work in progress at best. Though Payne was actively pursuing a probable hypothesis, a clearcut motive was certainly not established.

Even though Ronald Pope, the only identified suspect in the string of murders was himself killed, there was still a lot of good things to celebrate. Particularly in terms of how much access to critical information was at their disposal. The eyewitness, Mia Chisholm, verified the fake construction signage used on the van in Davidson's attack. Davidson's DNA was all over the back of the van. Brian Johnson, Alberto Sanchez, and several other unknown individuals' DNA was also located in the van.

The deeper they dug into Pope, the tighter the murders wrapped around him. Once they got access to his telephone, it was easy to track his whereabouts to the locations of the murders. It came as no surprise to anyone at that point when his phone tracked like clockwork to the scenes of all the homicides. The key focus for Payne was to identify Pope's partner in crime. Payne theorized that once Pope became a liability to their ritual of murder, he was masterfully outwitted and killed by his crony, his body left swimming in an ocean of evidence. Enough to convince the world Ronald Pope was a lone wolf. A lone crusader with an insatiable lust for murder.

"Once again, Detective Sergeant Payne and her dedicated team closed the curtains on another killing spree. You never fail to do the department proud," Lieutenant Lorrigan said as he walked by to his office.

Payne looked on in silence as Lorrigan entered his office. She soaked it all in for a second then sharply turned her attention back to her crew. Payne didn't mince words about the progress and future of the investigation. "This case isn't over. Not by a long shot. So, what do we know about our killers from the boat load of evidence we've processed?"

"The list of twenty-five names found on Pope's office computer all turned out to be well-known career criminals. That's not all. You'll never guess the first three names on the list. Davidson, Johnson, and Sanchez. What that really translates to is an unfinished kill list. A brutal work in progress," Hanson said.

"The overwhelming buildup of evidence compiled against Pope is quite telling. The stolen license plates found in his van and fictitious company logos were all key components of a masterful plot. A plan of deception and deflection away from the pile of broken bodies they left behind. What we don't know is why they're killing criminals?" Cruikshank said.

"Pope's cell phone placed him at all three murder scenes. Well, let me say it this way. His phone tracked to all three scenes where the bodies were recovered. It also put him at the location where Davidson was attacked and abducted. This, of course, supports the eyewitness account of him being there. There's absolutely no doubt we got the right perpetrator on this one," Hanson said.

"Pope's involvement is fully baked in. We can successfully clear all the murders on him for sure. The only concern would be the question of his partner, who remains unknown. Who was the man in the driver's seat of the van our witness spoke of? We don't yet know his full role or scope in any of this. Let's be clear, we're not talking about a one-off crime. This took months, if not years, of meticulous planning. This is a lot bigger than one man's doing," Toombs said.

"Okay, guys. Let's lean into the facts for a minute. First up, you're all right on the money about everything the evidence is saying to us. I'm unsure who's with me on this, but this is my take. Pope and his partner had a well-oiled murder machine going. They shared mutual motives in their abrasive murder enterprise. These men put lots of thought into their preparation. I mean, you have to give that to them. Their plan was probably as close to perfection as one could get. That was, of course, until Pope's sketch went public," Payne said.

"How do you plan to approach it going forward?" Toombs asked.

"By doing what we do best. We solve Pope's murder. Pope was killed by his partner in crime. I believe it's called self-preservation. The minute Pope's sketch went out, his days were numbered. That means the master manipulator is probably out there laughing at us right now. He knew it wouldn't be long until we pinched Pope. He must have known Pope would give him up when confronted with reality of the death penalty. So, he took care of Pope before we could squeeze any information out of him."

"Goddamn it. You sound like you know the guy. Like you can read his mind or something," Toombs said.

"Oh, yes, I know the guy. He knows we have nothing on him. He walked past our witness right here in this office, and she didn't blink. She had no idea who he was. The thought that she couldn't identify him only emboldened him. Goudy is the killer. He's the mastermind.

He was the man in the driver's seat that night," Payne said.

"Hold on a minute. You really wanna go that far with a gut feeling and circumstantial evidence? Can we prove any of this?" Toombs said.

"I may have found a way into his world, but it's going to take a little time. I wish I could say more, but I can't right now. In the meantime, work Pope's murder like our lives depend on it. See if there's any traceable connection between Pope and Goudy. Get out there and talk to people who knew Pope. Talk to his friends. Trust me, it's out there. We just need to find it," Payne said, slanting her head slightly.

Payne's little conference with her crew was closely followed by a briefing with Lt Lorrigan. One could accurately describe the mood in the briefing as less than enthusiastic or low energy. Nevertheless, Lorrigan was still flying above the clouds on the heels of the press briefing he gave over the weekend. His designation of Pope as the primary suspect in the string of murders was expected to help rekindle a sense of normalcy among the anxious citizens in attendance.

Knowing the man who brought terror to their streets was dead would definitely set their troubled minds at ease. It reinforced a sense of pride that their streets were safe to traverse once again.

Goudy had made it his mission to attend Lorrigan's press briefing. In fact, he was praised for his selfless work and contribution to surrounding communities. Goudy also received recognition for partnering with the police in the fight against crime. The pastor was touted as the kind of team player the city was proud to have and hoped to retain.

Payne gazed across the desk at Lorrigan, who seemed more composed than he had been for weeks. She assumed he must have gotten an encouraging response from somewhere. Whoever was responsible for Lorrigan's rapid mood makeover certainly created a positive turn in his recent sulky demeanor. The meeting with Payne and Lorrigan lasted only a few minutes. During their sit-down, Payne purposefully refrained from raising the name Goudy as the man responsible for orchestrating the murders.

The scrubbing of Pope's computer and telephone failed to identify any communication between Pope and the pastor. Nothing of evidential value on the devices pointed to Goudy or implicated him in any way.

Payne was convinced in her gut that Goudy being the kingpin. However, that carried little to no weight whatsoever in the eyes of the magistrate required to sign a search warrant. The requisite warrants to move on Goudy needed evidence of his involvement in criminal conduct. Unfortunately for Payne, she had nothing solid enough to present to a judge.

P ayne and Toombs headed out of the office for a sit down with Connie Wester, Pope's office assistant. Terrified that disgruntled citizens might turn their wrath for her deceased employer onto her, she skipped her residence of the past six years for a less conspicuous dwelling. The bland-looking house she sought refuge in was old and cold on the inside.

The lingering chills of winter seemed unusually apparent that Monday. That was a direct consequence of a slow-moving cold front drifting east through the city. Connie sat on a couch across from Payne and Toombs. With arms folded and legs crossed, Connie stared at the detectives through uneasy eyes. She showed no enthusiasm for entertaining house guests. Payne leaned into a probing look at Connie and read her mind like a tea leaf.

Payne softened her posture and slanted her cheeks before posing her first question to the timid little lady. "Connie, you came all the way out here to avoid being crucified by an angry mob? Pretty smart for an old bird like you."

"They won't accept the fact that I had nothing to do with my boss's madness, will they? No one in this city will hire me ever again. I'm stained for life. What good is a middle-aged woman scarred by the legacy of a killer?" Connie said, batting her eyes to fend off the flow of tears.

"If you're honest with them, they'll come around. I promise you this. Tell us everything you know about your boss, and in time, you'll have your dignity back," Payne said softly.

"I don't know what more to say. I already told the other detectives all I know. Don't you people talk to each other?"

"I read your statement. Connie, if we thought for a minute you had anything to do with Pope playing God, you'd be in an iron cage downtown. You've worked in that office for seven years. Trust me, you know a lot more than you realize. We have a few follow-up questions for you, then we're gone. Are we good?"

"Whatever you need. I have nothing to hide."

"Pastor Goudy from the Tabernacle, have you ever seen him and your boss together? Did they have any kind of business arrangement or personal relationship?"

"I've never seen that loudmouth flame thrower anywhere around the office. Something like that, I would remember. If those two had any relationship, they kept it to themselves. My boss was a private man. His personal life has always been off-limits."

"How private could he be? You've been around Pope long enough to know every time he passed gas. Give us something we don't know."

"When I say he was private, I mean everything about his personal life was hush-hush. The day he hired me, he made the terms and parameters of my employment crystal clear. I managed the front office, full stop. The computer in his office was for his use exclusively. I knew he had two cell phones. I've seen them countless times. I often wondered why he never gave me the number for the second phone. That wasn't my business anyway. After all, I was there to drink milk, not to count cows. I've always known he had secrets, but I never thought they were criminal. Now more than ever, I feel completely relieved he never considered me his confidant."

"Are you sure about the second phone? We only found one," Payne said.

"I'm sure of it. He never goes anywhere without them," Connie said.

"I guess the man who killed Pope made off with his second phone then," Toombs said.

"Goddamn it. He thought of everything. No wonder the son of a bitch is so cocky. Toombs, there's somewhere we need to be," Payne said, heading for the door.

T oombs peered over at his partner, who did nothing to disguise her growing frustration. Payne was livid at the idea of Goudy making this major mockery of the investigation. She believed he was rolling over Lieutenant Lorrigan like a lion toying with a lamb.

As far as she was concerned, that operational malfunction could not be allowed to stand for much longer. Not if she had anything to say about it anyway. More than anything else, she needed a win on this cunning clergyman.

He seemed to be ahead of the game at every possible turn. Evidence tying Goudy to Pope would give her the leg up she desired to break the clergyman's sneaky strides. Exactly the kind of evidence she believed Lattimore could provide. Payne merged onto Broad Street with her mind conditioned for her second sit down with Lattimore. Though the badly burnt man had admonished Payne on the first occasion, she surmised he might be willing to share a lot more than he projected with her.

CHAPTER EIGHTEEN

Payne flipped the indicator and veered off Broad Street onto the dirt road that led to Lattimore's junkyard. As she pulled closer and closer to the scrapyard's entrance, an ominous sensation gripped her in the gut. Of course, no one could decipher if her experience was strictly psychological. Nevertheless, the feeling that something was terribly wrong felt one hundred percent real to her. She looked across at her partner who instantly reciprocated. The visible stiffness of Toombs' eyebrows confirmed he understood her speechless call for caution. Payne refrained from feeding the truck anymore fuel. Instead, she quietly brought the truck to a complete stop.

Steady, but faint streams of smoke emitted from the half-open door and windows of the junkyard's front office. With pistols drawn, both detectives moved in through the unlocked gate. Whatever had triggered Payne's premonition of danger was quickly confirmed.

The smoky smell of death flowing from the office was unmistakable and profound.

Once inside, Payne's worst fears were immediately realized. Lattimore had been murdered. Burned almost to ashes right there in his unflattering little office. After living the greater part of his life fearful of fire, it was ironic his killer had chosen the flames to end his days.

The perpetrator could have easily burned the entire office to the ground, consuming all the evidence along with it. Instead, he made sure the fire was controlled and contained to the burning of Lattimore's body. It appeared the killer wanted everyone to bear witness to the horrors of his work.

Lattimore was restrained to a metal chair, doused with gasoline, and set ablaze. It is generally expected everyone will die once. The thought of Lattimore being set on fire twice in his lifetime would have been totally unthinkable until today.

"Payne, nothing you can do for him now. He's gone," Toombs said.

"Call it in. He was the link between Pope and Goudy. He knew their horrible history, and he was a part of it," Payne said.

"How do you know this guy? What else am I missing here, partner?"

"I intended to tell you about him. That's why I brought you here in the first place. His name was Lattimore. Nobody sees Goudy for what he truly is. That man is the personification of the worst among us. How does he even enter a church without first bursting into flames at the door? Instead, he preaches to others. Brother, this whole thing is way off the rails. It's just wrong," Payne said.

In short order, Julius and his crime scene crew rolled in and immediately got to work. A couple of minutes later, Doctor Sherman pulled up with his new assistant, Jacob Fields. This was Field's second stint with the Columbus Medical Examiner's Office. The first go around lasted until 2017, when he relocated to his home state of Texas.

In an attempt to resuscitate his waning relationship, Fields had moved to be with his wife. The fact that he was back in Ohio all by his lonesome was clear indication his marriage didn't turn out quite the way he wanted.

When Docter Sherman rehired his old pal, Fields expressed the view that it was better to have loved and fail than not to love at all. As much as Sherman showed an interest in Fields' personal life, he rehired him for one reason only. Fields was good at his job. He was as wide eyed and thorough as they come.

As the detectives sifted through the smoke-scented crime scene, Toombs stumbled on a huge jackpot. He found Lattimore's arm patch. The dirt-stained fabric seemed old and partially charred around the edges. Despite its shabby appearance, there was no doubt to anyone who its owner was. Similar to Pope's patch, below the One Law insignia, the initials ML were stitched in with blue thread.

Toombs saw the patch among a stack of old newspaper clippings. The items were buried like treasure under Lattimore's office couch seat.

Payne studied the patch carefully before turning her attention to the first newspaper article published by *The Columbus Sun*. The article was dated September 10, 1995. The names of five teenagers who suddenly went missing were the subject of the story. According to the article, they all disappeared within two weeks. The teens seemed to walk away and vanish into thin air. Ronald Pope and Michael Lattimore were prominently featured in the article. The other three teenagers were Eaton Byrd, seventeen years old, Karen Blunt, eighteen years old, and Chad Harrison, seventeen years old.

The light in Payne's eyes sparkled when she realized the significance of her partner's discovery. The invaluable pieces of evidence Lattimore inadvertently left behind for them to find provided enough reasons to smile. Any shrewd sleuth with more than a minute's experience would instantly recognize the find for the goldmine it was.

Mere days ago, the investigation was taking the detectives full steam ahead. The next thing they knew, things took a turn in an entirely different direction. The new trajectory pulled them back decades in time.

Payne preferred to continue following the natural flow forward, but the trail backward seemed far too alluring for her to ignore. This new turn afforded actual names of real people who could open doors into the hidden past of the One Law experience. Not only could they speak on what the group of missing teenagers had done, they could elaborate on who the individuals were. With those possibilities top of mind, Payne's priority was to quickly locate those individuals.

The second article Payne perused was published by the same newspaper two weeks earlier than the previous one. That story carried the caption, *Street Boys Disappeared Without a Trace.* The story painted a gloomy portrait of regular corner boys vanishing from the streets they frequented. Most of them had no one to report them missing. In many instances, those streets were the only home they knew.

Even if the likelihood the boys would live long enough to die of old age was slim, they weren't expected to suddenly up and vanish. Nevertheless, that wasn't the type of case that would inspire any massive manhunt. Some openly argued one required a permanent residence to be missing from. In many ways, the realities of the missing street boys' saga represented a much larger perspective surrounding the various tiers of justice that existed. How much emphasis is placed on individuals with high standing compared to persons of meager means?

H ours later, at the homicide office, Payne leaned on her team for the tremendous legwork it would take to ferret out the crucial evidence she sought. As she attempted to shed light on the most recent developments in the investigation, Detective McBride stomped into the office.

The mere sight of McBride stunned them all. His smile was like that of a creepy circus clown. His wristband from the hospital was still visible around his right wrist. Seeing McBride triggered wide eyes and open mouths among the detectives. Before they were able to muster any type of verbal response to his presence, McBride paused for a second. He gazed about, combed his hair with his fingers, then broke the ice with a tepid attempt at comedy.

"What's up with these looks? You stare at me like I just crawled from my coffin. Y'all realize I'm still alive, right?" McBride said, shifting gaze from one face to the next.

"You're damn right about that. For a minute there, I was pretty sure I was looking at your ghost. Why are you out of the hospital so soon, pal?" Toombs said.

"Straight for the jugular as usual. What if I say they released me early on good behavior?" McBride said, smiling like sunshine.

"John, what's going on? I know you have a long road ahead of you. I was there with you days ago, remember?" Payne said, closing the distance between them.

"I checked myself out of that cushy cuckoo's nest. You have to understand. I want to help you here. How can I sit on my ass while you guys are hard at work catching criminals? Sitting on my cheeks all day long is putting a real beating on what little sanity I have left. I need to work," McBride said.

"You have to trust me on this. The best thing you can do for us right now is get better. There will always be plenty of work to do, but there's only one John McBride. When the time is right, you'll have more than your fair share of work. This is not that time. This is a time for healing," Payne said.

Payne pulled out all the stops in her repertoire of words to persuade McBride to get the care he needed. It took a great deal of talking to convince him to check himself back into the hospital. McBride's expressed desire to reunite with his fellow detectives taking down criminals was predictably doomed, and they knew it. Watching his emotional decline was a rocky roller-coaster ride for his heartbroken colleagues who could do little more than observe from the sidelines.

Payne drove McBride back to the hospital and walked him inside. Despite the evolving urgency of the case, she felt duty-bound to prove to McBride that he wasn't alone. The safety and well-being of her colleagues have never been routine. To Payne, it was always considered personal and perhaps even obligatory.

After putting the McBride saga on ice, Payne doubled back to the homicide office. While she was out tending to McBride, Toombs used her absence to bring the rest of the team up to speed on everything they'd gathered from Lattimore's junkyard.

Cruikshank was already clicking away, scouring the files of missing persons from 1995. Hanson and Greenwood were busy tracking the whereabouts of the teenagers named in the newspaper articles.

Taking into account everything that occurred since Lattimore's vicious killing, Payne picked up the phone and dialed Daniel's number. After all, Daniel was the one who'd led her to the place where the first domino fell. What more did he know about the teenage outcasts from his past? Was there anything he'd forgotten to tell her that might lead to their current location?

The questions were many. On the other hand, the answers she sought often appeared challenging to find. After numerous attempts to reach Daniel on the phone failed, it became clear that her questions would have to wait for another time. It was one of those uncommon occasions where Daniel didn't immediately respond to her phone calls. The scenario drew a brief moment of pause during which Alyssa pondered Daniel's own personal safety. Wherever he was, and whatever prevented him from answering her calls, she hoped he was not in danger.

Payne massaged her cheeks and leaned into the chair in her office. She glanced at the picture of her dad on the desk and thought he appeared to look back at her. In that very instant, her phone rang. Before she had a chance to verify who the caller was, her troubled mind convinced her that it had to be Daniel calling her back. However, when she saw the name on the caller ID, her entire world turned upside down. All her thoughts of conversing with a friendly voice immediately vanished like a puff of smoke. Instead of finding a friend, she realized she had found a formidable foe.

"Detective Payne. Moments ago, while I presented the day's prayer, something dawned on me. I realized I didn't personally congratulate you and your hard-working team for a job well done. I'm compelled to admit my early skepticism until your unrelenting investigative skills won me over. Anyway, thanks for ridding our streets of the monsters who traffic in fear and folly," Goudy said.

"If anyone deserves credit, that would be you. As I understand it, you're the man who served up Pope on a platter a day after he was murdered," Payne said.

"Aw, Detective. Any good, law-abiding citizen would have done the same thing. There was really nothing special about my minor civic contribution."

"As for the real slippery killer. You know, the man who murdered Ronald Pope, I'm this close to clipping his wings. When I do, I'll make sure you're there to share in the celebration," Payne said.

"Good luck, Detective. I'll continue to pray for your success as always," Goudy said.

Tense was far too tender a word to describe the atmosphere during their coded conversation. The air was so heavy and dry that one's lungs could easily collapse under the rising tension. The undeniable reality that Payne and Goudy were deadlocked in a deadly high-stakes game of chess was slowly revealing itself in real-time for all to see. The smoldering embers were probably there all along, silently simmering under the surface. Intentional mind games masterfully disguised as genuine discourse. When one's liberty is at stake, there's no length one wouldn't go to conceal his crime. Consequently, there's no mountain Alyssa Payne wouldn't climb to capture any killer who found himself buzzing on her radar.

H anson and Greenwood got a little taste of success in locating the remaining three teenagers named in the old newspaper. Unfortunately, Chad Harrison drowned in a lake behind his house back in 2020. His death was ruled accidental and the case quickly closed. There was no witness to the incident and nothing suspicious snagged the interest of the investigators.

Eaton Byrd seemed to have overcome the difficulties of his youthful days and became a valuable member of the military. The challenge for Payne was that Byrd was said to be on classified deployment overseas and could not be reached. Based on what little they gathered, Byrd was some midlevel operative within the military. From the look of it, they may never get an opportunity to gain a glimpse of him, let alone interview him.

Everything rested on the shoulders of the only remaining teenager identified in the article. Karen Blunt instantly became their newest and brightest prospect in their delicate dig for dirt on Goudy. Karen worked at a cigar shop across town and still resided at her parents' home where she grew up.

Payne and Toombs were off in a jiffy devouring the road on their way to Karen Blunt's home. Little by little, Toombs started subtly acknowledging his initial reluctance to consider Goudy a criminal. His early assessment of the clergyman differed somewhat from that of his partner. Whilst Payne felt in her gut that Goudy was most likely more sinner than saint, Toombs felt more inclined to let him have the benefit of the doubt. Though his method would not be considered flawed, he began second guessing his lack of support for his partner's usually sound intuitions.

They drove down the driveway that led to the house. Dried-up and overgrown rose gardens sandwiched them from both sides of the unkept driveway. The seismic scope of neglect was difficult to ignore, yet their eyes instantly shifted to the woman who stood at the front door on the porch. Though both detectives had eyes on her, it wasn't until they stopped that they realized she was clutching a rifle. The raised barrel rested vertically against her thigh while its butt rested on the ground. The woman's awkward stance made her appear clumsy and confused. With Payne and Toombs looking on, no explanation was warranted regarding the likelihood of a loaded rifle finding itself in hostile hands.

The detectives' flow was steady and slow as they slid from the vehicle in front of the house. The woman tilted her head and sniffed the air. She turned eyes on the approaching sleuths. Her stare was as dreary and dead as a folklore duppy. She looked clean through them like they were transparent or perhaps too miniscule to see. The detectives moved closer to the woman before Payne announced their presence and presented their badges. Still, the daunting look of confusion remained present on the old woman's face.

"My ears may be lazy. These eyes don't see shit because of cataracts, but I can still send bullets up your asses," the woman said.

"What you say we cool things down a notch? I'm Detective Payne and this is my partner, Detective Toombs."

"I don't recall calling any detective; I have no need for cops. Last I checked, this was still private land. I could smell you riding the wind from miles off," the woman said.

Payne paused, searching for the right response to calm the old goose down. Suddenly, a younger woman came running through the rose bushes. She dashed between the detectives and mounted the steps to the front porch, shouting to the old woman to put away the gun. The minute she was close enough, she plucked the rifle from the old woman's grasp and laid it flat on the floor.

"Grandma, how many times do I have to tell you to stay away from that gun? What if you hurt someone? Do you realize you could have been shot today?" the younger woman said.

"Cops are like rats. They'll creep up quiet and piss in your coffee. I smell them both. I smell their sadness," the old woman said.

Payne eyeballed Toombs without uttering a word while the younger woman led the older one inside the house. Moments later, the younger woman emerged from the house and greeted the detectives. She introduced herself as Karen Blunt and apologized for her grandmother's behavior. She attributed her questionable conduct to the early onset of dementia that was eating away at her mind. According to Blunt, her grandmother's diminishing cognitive function had already claimed her job at the cigar shop as its first casualty. Blunt now resigned herself to being the full-time stay-at-home caregiver for her grandmother.

Once the meet and greet was played out and laid to rest, Payne went straight to the point of their visit. Right to the newspaper articles about the missing teenagers and what happened on the Walshes' farm. Perhaps there was something in Payne's direct approach that triggered an abrupt change in Blunt's attitude. The minute the Walshes' names were mentioned, she clammed up like she suddenly lost her tongue. When Payne reminded her that there was no statute

of limitation on murder, her tongue immediately loosened from its sudden vow of silence.

The light wind seeping in from the east carried a fresh
scent that softened the temperature a little. Payne's
flaming words scorched their way through Blunt's
world as they settled down on the porch. Even though
Blunt regained the compulsion to speak, it became
overtly apparent she wanted to avoid any conversation
about her past. Unfortunately for her, that wasn't a
compromise Payne was even remotely capable of ac-
cepting. Not at that pivotal point in the investigation.
Not when the past held the missing pieces required for
her to drop the hammer on her man.

"You do realize you're the only one left alive of the five
teenagers published in the newspaper article?" Payne
said.

"Look around. Everything is either dead or dying. I
already know death is coming for me. What about you?
Are you ready for it?" Blunt asked.

"We know there were street boys out there on the
Walshes' farm who the newspaper couldn't identify by
name. Lattimore told us quite a bit before he was murdered. Right now, we need you to tell us the names of
those boys. At least give us that," Payne said.

"Lucky for me, dementia runs deep in my family. My memory gets mighty blurry digging that deep into the past," Blunt said.

"Your memory is going to get a lot blurrier when you're rotting away in county lockup. Who's gonna care for Grandma then?" Payne said.

"Oh, that's really classy. Lattimore knew the rules before he went flapping his yap. Keep your mouth shut. That was the deal. Detective, I'm not fond of fire. Oh no. I've seen up close what the flames can do. As the last of the five, I know how to survive, and right now, I'm not fixing to fry for anyone. You get me? I have nothing more to say," Blunt said.

Toombs got to his feet and took a gander around the porch as he strolled from one end to the other. He picked up a pamphlet from the ledge at the far end. After flipping the page, he returned to his seat and handed the pamphlet to Payne. She scrutinized it, then flicked him a piercing glance.

Blunt sat there, soaking up the exchange between the detectives. Her expression suggested a complete metamorphosis of moods. Unease was perhaps the simplest way to describe the jitters that crept up and gripped her in an inescapable stranglehold. Gaping cracks broke wide open in her phony persona of confidence, making her appear exposed and vulnerable.

"This pamphlet is from the Guiding Light Tabernacle in Franklinton. It seems brand new. Karen, are you a member of that church?" Payne asked.

"Me? God no. You have no idea who you're messing with. You're going to get us all killed," Blunt said.

"So, you're not a member of the Tabernacle? How did the pamphlet get here then? Your old friend came by and paid you a visit? Did he rough you up some? You know, remind you to keep your mouth shut? Threatened to set you and crazy Granny ablaze like he did poor Lattimore? Come on, Karen. Talk to us," Toombs said.

"Is Pastor Vincent Goudy one of the street boys from the Walsh's farm?" Payne asked.

"Yes," Blunt said.

"Was he here?"

"Yes, Goudy was here. After all this time, he showed up two days ago. He warned me not to talk to you about him. To deny knowing him at all. See, I'm cooperating. Before I say another word, I need protection for me and my grandmother," Blunt said.

"Partner, we got him now. Let's get ready to bag that evil son of a bitch," Payne said, sticking a wicked stare on Toombs.

CHAPTER NINETEEN

B lunt coming clean about Goudy and Pope being a part of the group that murdered the Walshes signaled the beginning of the end for the slippery clergyman. That was Payne's personal take on the monumental progress they'd made in the case against him.

Night came quickly and covered the city like a damp blanket. Alyssa rolled in at the ranch but there was still no sign of Daniel. She knew he could be slippery whenever it suited him. That meant there was no immediate need to panic and send out a search party. She figured sooner or later, he would find his way home, hopefully still in one piece.

Payne's day had been long but fruitful. Karen Blunt gave a thorough account of her association with Goudy, Pope, Lattimore, and all the other members of the group from the Walshes' farm. She recounted a strong connection between Pope and Goudy from the outset.

Blunt recalled Pope following Goudy around as an obe-
dient pupil would his mentor.

Moments later, Alyssa's thoughts moved freely while
she soaked under the shower. The hot water beating
down on her shoulders delivered a well-timed dose of
physical therapy to the tension in her muscles. The only
thing she knew for sure was that it felt fantastic.

Wrapped in a towel, Alyssa sat on the edge of her
bed. She swallowed a sip of bourbon. The second she
rested the glass on the nightstand, her phone rang. Finally, Daniel decided to respond. Poised and ready to
pounce on her father for taking so long to return her
calls. She put the phone to her ear. However, once she
answered and heard the heaviness of his voice, everything changed in an instant. The obvious hysteria emit-
ting Daniel's mouth was more than enough to ignite her
attention.

"I found your last witness, but I was too late. Goudy
got to her first," Daniel said.

"What are you talking about, Dad? What witness?"

"I was following a solid lead all day for the last of
the five missing teenagers. That's why I couldn't take
your calls. Her name is Karen Blunt. I don't know, but
I got a bad feeling as I closed in on the house. A really creepy-looking place, I tell you. Then I saw Goudy's

Cadillac dusting away from the scene. Lyssa, the entire house was already up in flames when I got there. I couldn't do a damn thing to save her. Two teams from the fire department are cooling things down before they make entry, but I think it's pretty clear what they're going to find inside," Daniel said.

"Dad, Karen Blunt is alive and sucking air tonight, thanks to you. She's safe. Don't worry, you won't find her remains smoldering in the ashes. She's with us," Alyssa said.

"What? What do you mean she's with you? How did that happen?"

"We went to her house earlier today and met with her. She gave up all the goods on Goudy. We thought the safest place for her would be with us until we have Goudy in custody. If you took the time to pick up the phone, you'd be better informed about the whole thing."

"That is definitely the best news I've heard today. Thank God, you found her before that twisted son of a bitch. The minute he realized you were catching on to his shenanigans, he abandoned whatever little rationality remained in his rotten mind. He was always a madman murdering in the dark. Now that he knows he's about to be exposed, I would bet my last buck the ruthless bugger plans to go out with a bang," Daniel said.

"Well, there's nothing more for you to do at that smoke pit now. You better bring your butt home and get some rest. Tomorrow will be a big day for everyone. Once we have our ducks in a row, we pull the rug from under his feet," Alyssa said.

The dawning of a brand-new day came with the lingering realities of a homicidal madman who knew his brutal reign was nearing its end. That made him no less erratic and dangerous than a wounded animal in the wild, cunningly positioned and ready to pounce.

Having even the faintest insights into Goudy's twisted history should give any well-thinking person pause in their pursuit to capture him. Additionally, Payne needed no reminder of the persistent pushback she experienced from the powers above. Hence, her intended approach was to go by the book all the way to the end on this one. In terms of preparing the mounting evidence against Goudy, Payne planned on waiting until the noose was around his neck before moving in on him.

Payne's early morning sit-down with her crew at the homicide office was positive and energetic. Optimism was undeniably on display. Everyone actively played their specific part, putting the puzzle pieces together.

Karen Blunt's detailed statement fingered Goudy as the killer in the Walshes' cold case. She also laid out a clear connection between Goudy and the recently deceased Ronald Pope.

To make his dismal situation even worse, Goudy's recent threats on Karen Blunt's life marked a major turning point in his usually squeaky-clean public display. It placed the spotlight one step closer to his current involvement in criminal conduct as well as his attempt to conceal the crimes of his past. The most feasible conclusion to that situation was that he followed through on his threats toward Blunt. The fact that Daniel witnessed the slippery pastor fleeing the scene of the fire further solidified probable cause for the requisite search and arrest warrants.

"Arrest and search warrants for the untouchable Goudy are currently being prepared. Search warrants for his home, church, and phone. Finally, we're getting it all. The search will be slow and thorough. We need his DNA to analyze the evidence we already secured. The murder weapon is still out there, and it's about time we bring it in. There's plenty of forensic evidence to prove he worked with Pope to commit the murders; our job today is to find it," Payne said.

"I wish I could have been there to see the look on LT's face when you briefed him on Goudy's duplicity. It won't be a good look on him, being played by one of the most brutal killers of the century. Goudy's shit is splattered all over him now," Toombs said.

"You never know; you might still have that opportunity. I haven't briefed him yet. Actually, that's my next task of the morning," Payne said.

"Now I remember why I don't ever want your job. Anyway, avoid the fireworks today, please. We need cool heads going down the final stretch," Toombs said.

The crew looked on in relative silence while Payne went for her big sit-down with Lieutenant Lorrigan. Some may have anticipated endless headbutting and fireworks between the two. However, they had no alternative but to settle for a quiet day of dormancy.

Lorrigan leaned back in the chair and listened attentively while Payne outlined the recent progress in the investigation. This time, there was no pussyfooting around or second-guessing the fact that all roads led to Goudy being the mastermind for the murders. The look

on Lorrigan's face while he listened languished somewhere between hard defiance and the dread of defeat.

Payne could tell that the flames in his eyes burned
deep into his cranium. Though she garnered no pleasure watching her boss roasting on hot coals, it was
the unfortunate path of his own choosing. In fact, the
situation brought about a profound sense of sadness.
Deep down, she wished Lorrigan would find some kind
of soft landing in the end. After all, Lorrigan has always been a fair and steady hand to those under his
command. Truth be told, he was among the few in the
department she looked up to until his recent deviation
that left her scratching her head.

The second the briefing concluded, it was all hands
on deck, mustering the various teams for the raids on
Goudy. Payne requested a bird in the air for visual support and a dog on the ground. Nothing was being left
to chance for a man as devastatingly cunning as Goudy.
The dragnet needed to be sufficiently broad to contain
the suspect and remove any likelihood of escape.

The covert surveillance unit stuck on Goudy
overnight reported no movement from the prolific pastor. They were convinced he was still inside his home
after observing him enter the night before. It was
largely anticipated that Lorrigan's double-dealing may

cause him to sit out the operation. However, taking
into account the gigantic scope and significance of this
undertaking, being the unit's top cop necessitated his
presence on the ground.

The men and women on the tactical teams held
strategic positions with growing anticipation, waiting
for the tick of the clock and the signal to move in.
Hearts thumped like thunder inside their chests. Puls-
es pushed like dashing waves splashing back to shore.
The multitude of unknowns that followed the men and
women in law enforcement on their daily quest to serve
and protect could be difficult to comprehend at times.
Not knowing what awaits them on the other side of the
door can be a terrifying experience. Their jobs are not
for the faint of heart by any stretch of the imagination.
Those heart-stopping unknowns lived with them every
day on the job, stalking like a dreary shadow in the dark.
In their world, making it back home in one piece was
never guaranteed.

Lieutenant Lorrigan, being the man tasked with the
decision to move on this occasion, recognized the time
to go was imminent. Payne and Lorrigan made eye
contact; then Lorrigan gave the green light. From that
point, everything kicked into action. Lorrigan came out

in full tactical gear, removing doubt whether his head was in the game.

The major operation descended on Goudy's home. A more scaled-down contingent took control of the church in Franklinton simultaneously. The unmistakable melodies from Ricky Van Shelton's "To My Mansion In the Sky" played over and over again inside the house, but there was no response at the door when officers announced their presence.

The third call was the charm. The door was violently breached with the aid of a battering ram and entry made. Room by room, the building was cleared with the tactical team leading that charge. Payne pointed Toombs toward the source of the music and nodded for him to kill the noise and he did. After a while, it became apparent that no one was home. One noticeable message decorated the refrigerator in the form of a smiley face. The unflattering thing seemed crude like a sleepwalking three-year-old drew it. Nevertheless, the message was no less clear and chilling.

"This is not acceptable. I'm going to need a full account of this colossal fuckup from the surveillance team who sat on the house overnight. Where the hell is Goudy? With all this high-tech bullshit at their disposal, he just walked by them and vanished into the night. Is that what you're trying to tell me?" Payne said.

"If he really is our guy, we'll find the little shit. He overplayed his hand, and he knows it. Let him shake his ass all he wants, but he's done killing in this town. I want every cop in the city looking for him," Lorrigan said.

"Okay. Let our crime scene crew get to work. Everyone outside who doesn't need to be here. Let's go, people. We need Goudy's DNA analyzed right away," Payne said.

"That was Hanson on the phone. No sign of Goudy at the church either. He's in the wind, and he has a hefty head start," Toombs said.

"Don't worry your head too much about Goudy. He isn't going anywhere until he's done. His work is far too important for him to flee before it's finished. Let's compile the evidence. We'll continue to build the case against him until it's so tight it will strangle him just by him thinking about it," Payne said.

CHAPTER TWENTY

T he raids on Goudy's properties didn't conclude with the most-wanted pastor in custody but produced the next best thing, mounting evidence against him. Goudy's DNA acquired at his home during the raids turned out to be a definite match to the skin cells extracted from under Alberto Sanchez's fingernails. That damning piece of evidence was nothing short of a rosy treasure trove to the homicide detectives. It represented a crucial link between Goudy and the brutally murdered Sanchez. There's a saying out there that when it rains, it pours. Should that adage be believed, then it was raining tragedy for Goudy with no end in sight.

One cellphone was recovered at Goudy's home, and it was being analyzed by forensics. No documentation of evidential value was retrieved there, and there was no sign of the murder weapon. For a man with Goudy's level of culpability in at least four recent murders, his home was exceptionally clean. It appeared his ability to survive was definitely not by accident. His longevity relied exclusively on him being a meticulous murderer who planned every move with purposeful precision.

While the search at the church didn't yield the murder weapon either, they did recover two significant pieces of evidence there. His One Law arm patch bearing the initials VG was recovered in his office. They also found a one-page document Payne believed to be his mission statement for murder.

Payne and Toombs stood in front of the well-polished pulpit at Goudy's Guiding Light Tabernacle. The building was closed for business while the police searched for its elusive leader. As word circulated about Goudy's involvement, some started to describe him as the man who ran the most outrageous religious ruse in Columbus.

Payne studied the two exquisite golden stoups positioned on the wall at both sides of the pulpit. She was fascinated with them for a second until she snapped herself back on track. Payne pondered Goudy's motivation for violence given his daily teaching and continuous preaching for peace. Regardless of his treacherous childhood, he had clearly carved out a successful life for himself. What propelled him to cling so tightly to the demons of his past? Decades had gone by, yet he refused to relinquish his tainted ideology of vengeance and retribution.

"I thought I lost you for a moment back there. You just seemed miles away," Toombs said.

"I see it clearly now. This deluded archangel of death is even more twisted than we ever imagined," Payne said.

"What do you mean, partner? How so?"

"He actually thinks he's sending them off to a better place. Giving them a new life. He beats the living shit out of them then cleanses their broken bodies with baptism. The watermarks on the bodies that we couldn't explain; it's holy water from those shiny stoups on the wall. Goudy found a way to convince himself he's doing good by murdering those unrepentant career criminals," Payne said.

"Talk about a religious wacko. You're saying that in some homicidal way, he believes he's doing God's work? I wonder which God he's killing for? That's deep, even for you, Payne," Toombs said.

"This has nothing to do with me. Just study the evidence. Every decision he made was in furtherance of whatever he hoped to accomplish. Didn't you see his mission statement?"

"So, is he finished? I mean, now that his cover is blown, is it all over?"

"I'm afraid not. I don't think killing Pope was part of his plan. That was self-preservation. That was probably the only play to save his hide at the time. An opportunistic act of desperation to keep their killing machine moving along," Payne said.

"You knew all along he was bad news. How do you do it? How do you cut through the fog and figure shit out so easily?"

"Brother, I truly don't know what to tell you. Except I didn't know a damn thing. It was just a feeling. As a detective, you have to keep your nose to the ground and follow that scent. Never get distracted by those without the taste for it. Just keep on going wherever it takes you," Payne said.

The homicide office was kicking with activities surrounding the search for Vincent Goudy. Whether out of personal embarrassment or unblemished concerns for the community's safety, the expression on Lieutenant Lorrigan's face said he needed the Goudy saga to be concluded forthwith. Behind bars or into the ground, either way, he wanted the stench of Goudy gone from him for good.

Payne used the time to strategize with her team to unravel Goudy's location and figure out who the bone-crushing pastor planned to murder next. While they waited for information from Goudy's phone to come in, they continued working other means of tracking him down.

There was no activity on any of Goudy's credit or debit cards. No withdrawal or attempts to shift funds from his financial accounts. His picture was shown across television networks and plastered on the front pages of every local newspaper in town. Not simply as a person of interest but as the primary suspect in multiple murders. In a matter of hours, the famous Pastor Goudy's unblemished reputation plummeted.

"Alright, everyone. This is where we are. There's no more skirting around the obvious. Vincent Goudy is the primary suspect in the four murders we're currently working. The thing is, he's on the run and holed up somewhere right here in this city. You have all seen how brutally deadly he is, and I don't think he planned on leaving the city alive. I also don't believe he intends to go quietly or without taking casualties along with him," Payne said.

"The earliest intelligence we gathered on him took us back to 1995, when he was a teenager living on the street. He and other runaway teenagers were taken in by the Walshes on their farm in the woods. We all know the rest of that story. He murdered the Walshes and burned the buildings to the ground with the aid of the other teens," Toombs said.

"Goudy vanished from sight immediately following the killings. No one knew where he went or where he came from originally. No one knows if Goudy is even his real name," Payne said.

"The next time anyone saw him was in 2013, when he reappeared from God knows where and started the Guiding Light Tabernacle in Franklinton. Goudy is no simpleton. He must have envisioned this day might come when he'd need a place to lay low. That means he must have prepared for it. If we're going to find this killer, we need to know who he really is," Toombs said.

"He thinks he's the angel of death. Based on this mission statement we recovered at the Tabernacle, they think thieves exist to kill and destroy. Goudy is trying to rid the world of habitual criminals who refuse to turn their lives around voluntarily. When people fail to accept his preaching, he breaks their bones and saves their souls through baptism. He coordinated well with the bondsman to identify the worst criminal offenders to select," Payne said.

"How in hell were these madmen allowed to carry out those vicious executions and escape police attention? Far as anyone can tell, there could be more undiscovered bodies out there somewhere," Hanson said.

"We know a whole lot about these horrible men, but there's still plenty we don't understand. So, put on your thinking caps and let's dig up their buried secrets. By the end of the day, I want to know more about Goudy than the twisted bone breaker knows about himself," Payne said.

Payne suspected Goudy was most likely hunkered down in his secret bunker or safehouse somewhere off the grid. Running around trying to leave the city in the middle of a manhunt might not have been a prudent option for the criminal mastermind. The fact that they didn't find the murder weapon nor other incriminating evidence at Goudy's house further suggested he had a hidden hole to hide in.

With his picture posted all over the media, they were hopeful someone would recognize him entering or leaving his lair and call in a tip. Goudy was undoubtedly shrewd in his scheming and manipulation of others. Regardless of his buoyancy, he still wasn't invisible. The detectives were banking on the likelihood that some-one must have seen something. Goudy's ability to oper-ate below the radar undetected by no means rendered him a ghost. What it did was reiterate his proficiency at shady gymnastics. A modern-day Houdini when it came to committing murders and giving the authorities the slip.

P ayne sank into the comfort of her leather chair. The office lights were dimmed, and the blinds were partially drawn. Anger and frustration roiled within her as she obsessed over everything that had happened. She let her mind run wild for a few min-utes, but then she pushed to her feet, knowing that she wouldn't accomplish anything just sitting on her butt.

With a resolute look, Payne traded the shadowy con-fines of her office for the freedom of the open floor. No sooner had she stepped out than Cruikshank shouted for her. His obvious elation drew the crew together like a swarm of ants to a stick of candy.

The data from Goudy's phone had come in from the forensic technicians. They quickly learned that calls and texts from the phone appeared limited to church business. Which was probably why Goudy deliberately left it behind for them to find. He knew full well they wouldn't discover anything incriminating about him.

Goudy was still taking precautions though the cops already had more than enough evidence stocked up against him to bury him for life. Regardless of the minimal usage of the phone for criminal communication, Cruikshank was more excited about coordinates from its previous geographic locations.

"This better be good. Okay, talk to me," Payne said.

"At first glance, it's all useless chatter. Where things get interesting is when we line up the phone next to Pope's. They both pinged like twins. It's clear that Pope and Goudy were together at the murder scenes and dump sites. More and more, the case against Goudy is proving to be ironclad," Cruikshank said.

"Is there anything to help us ascertain Goudy's current location? That's the big question. Goudy's culpability is already in the bag, as far as I'm concerned. What we need to do is find the fucker now. We need to get him in our sights before he drops another body as a parting gift," Payne said.

"We're looking at every cell tower the phones pinged on. Coupled with their vehicle's navigation, we might have a shot at something. Give it a little time, and we'll have possible locations to get eyes on," Cruikshank said.

"Goudy is a real-life ghost if you ask me. We turned over every rock you could think of and couldn't find a single trace of Vincent Goudy. Theres nothing on record of where he came from. No indication where he disappeared to following the Walshes' killings. It seems like the name Vincent Goudy was an ingenious invention of that bone-crushing madman," Greenwood said.

"At the moment, time is an invaluable commodity we have little of. While we wait for you to sniff out his hideout, here's what I need you to do. Talk to Goudy's employees. Hear what his beloved congregants have to say about their tainted messiah. When he sneaked out of his house and slipped the surveillance team that night, he didn't vanish into thin air. Go back over street cams in the vicinity. I'll go have another word with Karen Blunt and see if she remembers anything else. Come on, guys, get me something to go on," Payne said.

CHAPTER TWENTY-ONE

V oid of any light from the timid moon, darkness prevailed unabated along the outskirts of the ranch. Candid conversations between Daniel and Alyssa were sobering as the father-daughter duo deliberated on possible places Goudy might have chosen to hide.

Daniel reminded Alyssa that criminals who are mentally invested in their motives were significantly more inclined to revisit the scenes of their crimes. Their almost parental connection with their victims often extended to locations and personal apparel, including valued belongings.

Looking back over Goudy's dedication to the murders, in Daniel's view, he checked all the boxes as the kind of killer who would want to be close to the scenes of his crimes. Perhaps Alyssa needed a different perspective. A necessary reminder of the type of monster who had come from unknown beginnings and trans-formed Columbus into a chilling killing field.

A s Alyssa slept into the night, the rare moment of rest for her was like a dose of healing tonic to her ailing body. Much like a healthy heart needs to beat, a constantly working body requires sufficient sleep to function at its optimum. That neglected necessity was among the things Payne often pushed aside to facili-tate her relentless desire to bring her cases to successful conclusions. A selfless act of self-sacrifice in pursuit of the greater good.

Though well intended, it was unsustainable and des-tined for doom. Candles that burn too bright tend to burn out quickly. Though Payne might be in the best shape of her life at the moment, persistent disregard for self-care is predictable for problems further down the road.

Payne slept like a baby in heaven until the ring of her phone abruptly awakened her. She answered and soon recognized the loaded voice of the killer at the other end. Without taking even a second to think, Payne dialed Toombs' number from the landline in her room. She placed the phone close enough for Toombs to hear her conversation with the killer on the other end. The minute Toombs figured out the play, he called in a trace on Payne's phone. The objective of the trace was to ascertain a fix on Goudy's location without him knowing the detectives were on to him.

"Detective Payne, you of all people should know better. The heights of power reached by great men were not attained by sudden flight, but while their companions slept, toiling upward in the night," Goudy said.

"Is this your sick idea of a joke? What is this game you're playing? Why call me at 3:25 a.m. and recite poetry in my ears?" Payne said.

"How could you be sleeping while the most brutal killer of your lifetime runs loose in your city? Isn't that how you try to color my character through your gullible media outlets? You showed not one lick of respect for the quality of my work. You knew better, yet you distorted the very nature and purpose of my service to this beloved city. For that, Detective Payne, there's a price you will pay."

"Stop this madness right now. Turn yourself in. End this frigging fiasco without further anguish or bloodshed. You made your point quite convincingly. Now it's time to come in," Payne said.

"Aha. Is that so? Time to come in? Come on now, Detective. Turn myself in you say. How can I? Don't act like that clueless lieutenant at your office. He's always a day late and a dollar short. You, more than anyone, should understand why I can't turn myself in. Not after you and your overzealous colleagues trampled on my reputation and shit at the altar of my legacy. Now it's time for me to hold your feet to the fire. This is definitely not the kind of finale I envisioned, but it's going to be you and me at the end, Detective Payne. You and me," Goudy said, dropping the phone on the ground and slipping away into the night.

Zeroing in on the address Goudy called from presented little to no challenge to the tech team, considering that he left the phone line alive like an open invitation. That simple act of carelessness was definitely a taunt, given his demonstrated level of proficiency with technology. Within minutes, they confirmed he called Payne from Lattimore's junkyard.

Patrol units in the vicinity rolled quickly to the junkyard but Goudy was long gone by then. Goudy's phone was retrieved outside the front office where he dropped it. The entire place was searched but except for his phone, nothing else indicated he was even there.

Payne wasn't the least surprised by the outcome. In fact, she was even more convinced the deadly pastor was setting her up for a cynical game of cat and mouse. With that in mind, she snuggled under her blanket once again and went back to bed.

B irds bestowed their beautiful ballads from the comfort of their high perch. Payne was up on her feet at the crack of dawn, joining her feathered friends ushering in another glorious Columbus morning. Notwithstanding the sweetness of the melodious music from the chirping songbirds, the only thing on Payne's mind was apprehending Goudy and bringing him to justice.

Payne's dismantling of the archangel's spiritual hierarchy precipitated his rapid decline to nothing more than a narcissistic despot. A ruthless religious fanatic with a heavy hand and a violent heart. A man with the knowledge and expertise to do good, who instead devoted himself to a secret life of vengeance and murder.

L ieutenant Lorrigan appeared even grumpier than usual this morning, if that was possible. Of course,

he had reasons to be mindful of the multiple bel-
ly-blows constantly jabbing away at his precarious reputation. Whenever Goudy's name got mentioned in internal reports or publicly in the media, it mirrored a
negative light right back at his feet.

Ironically, the thing Lorrigan found most reprehen-
sible wasn't his mistake of dealing with the killer. Instead, he deflected his rage toward Payne for putting
Goudy front and center in the public eye and keeping
him there. Payne's persistence in bringing killers to justice made it abundantly clear the Goudy investigation
wasn't going away until he was placed in bangles or a
box.

Payne took one look at Lorrigan's demeanor and
switched direction toward her office. A pointless boxing bout with her boss was definitely not on her list
of activities for the day. Her sights were squarely set
on catching a deranged killer, not dillydallying around
petty workplace politics.

Though Payne's intention was to avoid an unwarranted confrontation with Lorrigan, there were certain aspects of his temperament she couldn't ignore.
There was no way around wondering whether he would
rather have Goudy in a body bag than handcuffed in
the back of a squad car. A narcissistic killer flapping his

mouth could make prevailing circumstances a lot more difficult for the embattled Lieutenant. Before Payne had the chance to drop into her chair, Cruikshank called her out on the floor.

"This better be good. What about the street cams you should be surfing? What's the story there?" Payne said.

"That's the reason I called you out. Sadly, there's still no sign of Goudy on any of the previous cams I've seen. However, I found something from last night I think might interest you," Cruikshank said.

"You have my attention. Show me what you got," Payne said.

"Take a look at this old Toyota pickup. This was two blocks from Goudy's house the night he ditched surveillance. The problem is that we can't make out the driver from this angle. To make matters worse, we only have a partial on the plate," Cruikshank said.

"Am I missing something? What about that old pickup truck makes it so interesting?" Hanson said.

"Hold on to your tickets; the show isn't over yet. This is the same pickup caught on cams last night. Less than a quarter mile from Lattimore's junkyard. Doesn't this look like Goudy in the driver's seat? This time we also have a clear view of the license plate," Cruikshank said.

"You're a Goddamn genius. That's what you are. A crafty little genius. What about the plate? Is it any good?" Toombs said.

"The plate is unassigned. I tried digging for info on it and came up light. My guess is the plate may be as old as the pickup, if not older. There was no other sighting of Goudy or his truck for the rest of the night," Cruikshank said.

"This is solid work. Good job, Detective. Now that we know what his ride looks like, make sure all eyes are looking for it," Payne said.

"Are you going to let the LT in on this break? He's going to blow a gasket if you don't bring him up to speed on something this big," Toombs said.

"I'm about to brief him. Whatever we learn going forward, make certain I'm the first to know about it," Payne said.

Lorrigan immediately threw heat on the street. Tactical teams and every available body he could muster became a part of the manhunt. The streets were saturated with cops looking under every rock they could imagine.

As time progressed and momentum waned, at the end of the day there was little positive to report back. Anxiety wore thin among many while the elusive Goudy remained in the wind. The brightness of day dimmed and slowly slithered away, enabling the rustic color of evening to drift in and parade its presence. Somewhere in those fading moments of the day, Payne and Toombs got in the truck and took to the streets. Payne revisited Lattimore's burnt-out junkyard without any clear reason for doing so. She just wanted to be at the place Goudy called her from.

"Why did the twisted bastard want me to know he was calling me from here? The place he murdered Lattimore. He knew I would come," Payne said.

"Sounds to me like he's all the way up in your head. Are you inside his head too? Don't let him pull you under his hammer. You gotta be careful with this guy," Toombs said.

"You know, Dad said something to me last night, and it never felt truer. He said killers like Goudy always return to the scene of the crime."

"Well, he was right on the money about this one. Maybe he could set up a shop at the ranch and tell fortunes. You know, read palms and shit like that."

"Is everything always a joke to you? Can't you be fucking serious for once? I'm trying to think like a killer in order to catch this freaking killer, and you think it's okay to drop jokes."

"You have the right to think I'm an ass, but I'm just trying to make you laugh again. Goudy pulled you too far up his tailpipe. I want to make sure the partner I knew still resides inside of you."

"I'm right here where I'm supposed to be. Just quit that squirmy stuff and think about Goudy's next move. Straighten your shit out, and I promise you we'll get him."

"No need to elaborate any further. How can I help?"

"Which one of Goudy's crime scenes would give sufficient coverage for a hideout? It must be secluded enough to keep the old pickup concealed and undetected," Payne said.

"Don't tell me you believe he has balls that big to set up shop at his own murder scene? Nobody does that."

"Goudy spent his entire life hiding in plain sight. Parading in front of the whole world. There's no telling what narcissists like him would or wouldn't do. They get off by living on the edge. By doing the unexpected. That's how he survived," Payne said.

"I'm going to have Cruikshank look over possible locations connected to the crime scenes. Also, did any of the victims or their relatives own an old pickup?" Toombs said.

Toombs and Payne were about to leave the junkyard when Payne received a call from Daniel. He saw Goudy in the old Toyota pickup on the front page of *The Columbus Sun*. Daniel took one look at the picture and remembered the Walshes owned a pickup identical in model and color. Pictures of the pickup were captured in the Walshes' crime scene photographs taken back in 1995.

A quick check revealed that the license plate on the pickup featured with Goudy was a perfect match to the one from the Walshes' crime scene photos. Payne grilled Daniel about habitable building structure at the Walshes' farm, but nothing he recalled suggested rehabilitation of the charred ruins there. As far as Daniel knew, the buildings were burned to rubble. Having no known offspring to carry on the legacy, the farm was left abandoned. Due to the property's tragic history, citizens back then kept their boundaries and stayed clear of what was referred to as the Walshes' accursed farm.

"Buckle up. We're going for a ride," Payne said.

"According to your old man, there's nothing left at that burn pit but ghosts and shrubs. You'll need to hustle to reach that wilderness and back before nightfall," Toombs said.

"You're right. There might be nothing out there, but I have to be sure. I need to satisfy myself. Goudy wasn't hiding right under our noses all this time. The Walshes' farm isn't very far away from the scene where Sanchez was beaten and murdered. He probably perched in the shadows and watched us process the crime scene that evening," Payne said.

There was a rustic red in the skyline while the departing sun indulged in mortal battle with the drifting clouds. As the detectives veered off the main road to the Walshes' farm, they quickly observed fresh tire tracks.

Toombs suggested calling for backup but Payne opted to wait until they verified what was out there. A mile in, they came upon a daunting sign nailed to a tree. It read, *Private property. Trespassers will be shot.* Payne perused the sign, paused for a moment, and eyed her partner. Toombs pulled his Glock from the holster and placed it in his lap as they proceeded farther. A minute later, Toombs pointed to a house up ahead. The Toyota pickup was parked under a shed facing out.

Payne gazed at the fading sun that seemed locked in a hopeless battle with the approaching night. She pondered the significance of where they were to the killer they pursued. It was the place where Goudy felt his first thirst for blood. The very spot he practiced with his first two kills.

Payne peered up at the mystical sky that appeared poised to cry. The approaching darkness seemed to shadow the flaming sky in a red silhouette. In some almost magical way, the entire picture was a painter's masterpiece. The gray house on the hill surrounded by giant trees. The makeshift shed with the Walshes' old pickup peeping out. The two detectives waiting to collide with the city's most prolific killer. It was a breathtaking spectacle for a portrait though it swirled above the crime scene of the dead. It was an absolute travesty to think that a picture so magnificent may forever be construed as the red silhouette of death.

Payne called in for backup as they slid from the truck. Their pistols were drawn and positioned at the ready. What they found there in the middle of nowhere was a sure shocker. Goudy had joined two huge containers and converted them into the perfect hideaway house.

The layout of the camp appeared skillfully organized from a defensive standpoint. From the look of it, one could live there for years without the need for anything. The house was completed with an overhanging roof and catchment for water that fed into a tank. The smell of meat cooking on a smoker out front clearly indicates the bloodthirsty pastor was home.

Clouds in the bloodred sky stood still. An uneasy stint of silence sank in and seemed to swallow everything. Payne had no doubt their presence was known, and she had no intention of leaving without her man. The detectives made their way closer to the house. Payne secured the front while Toombs cautiously inched his way around back. Payne knocked then tried opening the door, but it was locked.

"Vincent Goudy, this is the Columbus Police. Open the door and show yourself. No need to prolong the inevitable. You had a lengthy run, but it's over now," Payne said.

"Detective Payne, aren't you a pesky little devil? You couldn't be satisfied with the bloated bondsman? You had to hunt me down like a common criminal, didn't you? Now, here we are about to rip each other apart like rabid dogs," Goudy said.

"Vincent, no one needs to die here today. The ball is in your court now. Open the door and let's do this face to face. Is that all you can do, crawl from behind like a coward and attack your unsuspecting victims? Come on, grow two stones and open the door."

An extended pause ensued. Nothing anywhere but empty silence. Suddenly, a loud commotion around the back and a bellow from Toombs. Payne yelled out to

Toombs and got no response. She rushed to the back of the house and found Toombs knocked out cold on the ground. Goudy had wacked him good from behind with his beloved iron bat.

Payne called to him but he was far from conscious. She crouched over him and attempted to check his pulse. Before she ascertained whether Toombs was alive or dead, Goudy came upon her from behind. She started to turn but quickly acknowledged the pastor had beaten her to the draw. He had Toombs' Glock locked on her in an offensive stance. He moved swift and light on his feet like he was having the time of his life. They both froze in limbo for a moment with fiery eyes fixed on each other. Goudy shook his head, suggesting she not try anything shady.

"Slowly now. Please, lose the steel. Drop it in the tank. You won't be needing that anymore. Now that I've grown two stones, let's settle things face to face," Goudy said, with triumph and bluster in his delivery.

"You got rid of my gun already. Please, let me check on my partner. If he dies, they'll take you to the chair for it. So far, you haven't hurt a cop. Don't start now," Payne said.

"I have no fear of your electric chair. My work that you've toppled is more powerful than you could ever begin to fathom. Look at the flaming red sky. It is bleeding for your spiritual ignorance. I told you there's a price for your interference. Tonight, you and your wounded sidekick will pay with your lives."

"You think I don't understand why you murdered those career criminals? Well, I do. They were hardened criminals. Still, they were not insects for you to squash like cockroaches."

"It's not murder if it's God's will."

"You think because you doused them with your so-called holy water that you're saving their souls? You call that bullshit blasphemy a baptism? Come on, man. That's deranged and desperate. Even for a crazy fanatic like you."

"That's not a smart way to beg for your lives. When your body hits the ground, I will wash you clean and set your soul free just like I did them."

"I won't beg. You're going to kill us anyway. This will be the last time you attempt to play God. After today, if there's a hell somewhere out there, you'll rot in it."

"Any last word before I send you home?"

"Just let me check on my partner. Let me say goodbye to him," Payne said.

"Go ahead. Say your piece, but make it quick," Goudy said.

Payne soaked in a long look at Goudy before slowly kneeling over Toombs. Goudy stood there with a cynical smile and a look of death in his eyes. As she turned her attention to Toombs, Goudy hummed away at his favorite tune, "Mansion in the Sky."

At that moment, Payne knew it was do or die. Slowly, she felt for Toombs' second piece in his ankle holster. Once she had a hold of the gun, she paused for a second then did what had to be done. She turned to face her executioner and rolled thunder on him. She blasted six rounds into the flabbergasted preacher. He skipped and danced agonizingly to the bite from each burning bullet. His hideous death dance mimicked the antics of a frightened child being stung all over by scorpions. Finally, his lifeless corpse hit the ground next to the Glock and his iron bat.

The sound of sirens singing in the distance meant the calvary was swiftly swooping in. Toombs had suffered a concussion accompanied by a headache he couldn't wait to forget. Within seconds, the camp was overrun by an anxious army of cops. Medics tended to Toombs, who was quickly on his feet and eager to break free of them.

Lorrigan rolled on the scene like a man on a mission. The minute Payne informed him of Goudy's demise, the beauty of life glittered in his eyes once again. For the first time in weeks, Payne saw the lieutenant smile.

The redness in the sky gradually turned to gray. The spectacle of a star-filled night stepped in and devoured what remained of the day. The terror and torment of the bone-crushing killers was gone for good from the streets of Columbus.

There was one phone call Payne needed to make before she headed home. She called Fabian Davidson's mother to inform her they got her son's killer.

Two cold ones at the ranch seemed the perfect way to bring closure to an extraordinary day, her way of closing the curtains on the most cunning killer to plague Columbus for decades.

Made in United States
Orlando, FL
26 December 2024

56503409R00143